Bonnie
Yr 6

THE YOUNG EXPLORERS
AND THE
SWORD OF QUEEN MARTHA

By Neil Jones
Illustrations by Catherine D'Arcy

AUDLEY
BOOKS

Published in the United Kingdom by:
Audley Books
12 Audley Road,
Colchester,
Essex CO3 3TY

ISBN 978-0-9554387-0-7

A CIP record of this book is available from the British Library.

Printed by:
Lavenham Press Ltd,
Arbons House,
47 Water Street,
Lavenham,
Suffolk. CO10 9RN

Design and Layout by David Turner

To our own young explorers,

Emma, Bonnie, Daisy, Ella, William and Alec

COMING SOON!!

THE YOUNG EXPLORERS AND THE
CURSE OF BLICKLING HALL

www.theyoungexplorers.co.uk

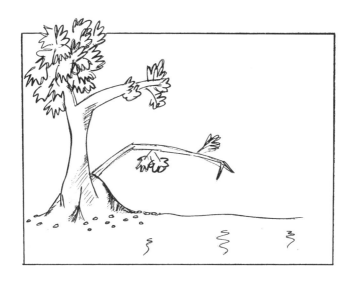

Chapter One

The final bell at the end of the school day is a rather wonderful sound. Even better is the bell that sounds the end of term.

But perhaps the best bell of them all is the one that heralds the start of the summer holidays, and it was that one Jim was excitedly listening out for.

As the clock plodded slowly around to 3 o'clock he kept turning to his pal Robert and smiling.

Robert smiled back because, like Jim, he knew what the ringing of that bell meant, six weeks of freedom, six weeks of making dens, sailing boats and best of all six weeks of swimming.

For the last three years, Jim and Robert had marked the start of the school summer holidays with a swim in the River Colne. As soon as that bell rang they would sprint back home, grab their shorts and then cycle down to the riverside. Whatever the weather, they would rest their bikes against a nearby bush and then climb the 'springboard', the name they gave to a rather large tree that stooped over the water's edge like an old man who had just dropped a coin.

The 'springboard' was a little way down the path from the village but it was well worth the trip. It had a number of thick, huge branches that swung across the river, providing perfect platforms for young boys to jump off.

In the last year, Jim and Robert had perfected their leaps. They had even moved on to proper dives, although because of the shallowness of the water they had to move further along the branches to make sure they plunged in somewhere deeper.

Such fun could not be contained by two excitable young fellows and despite a vow to keep the 'springboard' secret, the unbounded joy of leaping off a tree into the river soon got out.

And so it was on that particular day Robert and Jim were joined by Peter and Andrew.

After school, the four friends met up in the school playground and agreed a meeting point by the station. They then went their separate ways back to their homes to grab swimming shorts and their bikes.

Jim was first at the station closely followed by Robert. The other two were slightly late, only by a matter of minutes, but despite the short period of time Jim and Robert were still looking to leave without them. The excitement was just too much.

"Come on you two," Jim called out to them. "We've been waiting ages."

"I had to tell my mum where we were going," Peter replied.

"And we're not that late," Andrew added.

"Who cares, you're here now," Robert said and then pointed towards the estuary. "The path is down there."

Peter froze. "You didn't say we were going to Dragon's Hill."

"We're not you big girl," Jim said angrily. "It's down by the river. No where near the woods."

"My dad says it's not safe there. There was this woman who…"

"Yeah, yeah," Jim interrupted him. "We've all heard the story. Flipping heck Pete either you want to come swimming, or you don't."

"I thought it was by the shipyard."

"Well it isn't," Robert told him, now also getting a bit cross.

Peter was seriously eating into their swimming time with all his worrying so Robert gave him an ultimatum.

"Right we're going now. It's up to you Pete."

So Peter went with them.

A few minutes frantic cycling up the path and they were soon at the 'springboard'.

As Jim and Robert quickly got off their bikes Peter and Andrew looked up at the imposing tree.

"You jump off that?" Andrew said.

"Yep, it's brilliant. Look, watch me," Jim said hurrying towards the tree and climbing up the trunk to the first branch. A few more steps higher and he was a good 20 feet up. He slowly made his way out over the water and then suddenly jumped yelling yippee!

Robert followed him and made a similar spectacular leap before Andrew was convinced it looked fine and also joined in.

As all three splashed about in the water Peter nervously watched from the riverbank.

"What are you waiting for Pete, the water's great," Andrew called out to him. Then he turned to Jim. "I'm going back to try and persuade him to come in."

So Andrew swam back to the water's edge and got out. Dripping wet he told Peter there was nothing to worry about and led him to the tree.

"It's a breeze."

Peter wasn't sure but knowing he would be called a sissy for the rest of his school life if he didn't jump, decided to climb up the tree alongside Andrew.

As the two of them sidled out along the branch Jim and Robert shouted encouragement from the water below.

Peter looked down and took a deep breath. He had finally decided to do it, and was just about to jump, when he heard a blood curdling screech coming from the woods behind him.

"What the hell was that?" Andrew said turning around, but as he did he slipped on the branch and started to tumble.

Automatically he tried to grab hold of the nearest thing to steady himself, which unfortunately was Peter.

Both of them fell horribly off the branch and plunged into the river with an almighty splash.

Andrew was the first to emerge, spluttering slightly and Peter was quick to follow.

Jim and Robert laughed, relieved that their friends were safe.

"Well at least you're in now Pete," Robert called over to him.

Peter smiled and began swimming over to his friends before something grabbed hold of his legs and dragged him under the water.

Andrew was bobbing up and down right next to him but didn't see or hear a thing but Jim and Robert did, and called out to him immediately.

Andrew spun round but Peter was nowhere to be seen. He had completely vanished beneath the ripples.

"I can't see him," Andrew cried out in panic, searching all around.

Jim and Robert started to swim towards him but within seconds Andrew was gone too.

"Andrew," Robert yelled. But it was no good. Just like Peter he had been swiftly dragged under with a force so brutal it was over in a second.

Stunned, the colour quickly drained from the faces of Jim and Robert as they gently drifted in the water not really knowing what to do. They looked at each other in horror and then turned to face where Peter and Andrew had both been seconds earlier. Surely they would both come up for air in a minute.

And then it dawned on them they would not.

Robert's heart began to pound and he felt himself gasp for breath. 'Oh my god' he thought. He was next. Whatever it was that got Peter and Andrew was coming for them, he knew it. He suddenly felt something brush past his leg and yelped.

"What?" Jim yelled, also petrified they were about to meet the same fate.

"Something just ..."

"It was me."

"Oh."

They knew it wasn't safe to stay in the water so without saying a word, and in a blind panic, they both swam like they had never swam before, frantically flaying their arms through the water as fast as they could.

Panting heavily, they pulled themselves up and back on to dry land and as soon as the relief set in Robert began to cry.

"We didn't even look for them Jim."

Jim put his arm round him.

"There was nothing we could do."

He knew there was no use looking for their friends. They were gone forever and as the days turned into weeks, and the weeks turned into months it turned out they would never be seen again.

Chapter Two

"Shush please."

The librarian of Wellsbridge College was starting to get a bit annoyed with the group of students at the far end of the oak beamed reading room.

Drake Young on the other hand was more than grateful for the distraction.

She had been sitting quietly at the other end of the 16th century study area reading a book she knew all too well she was not allowed to touch, let alone read.

It was Kensie's Historie of the Ancient British Tribes and it was more than 400 years old.

Only the most important professors of the college were allowed access to the book and the only reason Drake was now leafing through it was that her parents were perhaps the most important professors of the lot.

As joint heads of Archaeological Studies at Wellsbridge, Charles and Mary Young were very highly regarded. Whatever book they wanted, they could get. So it seemed only fair that as their daughter, Drake should be given the same privileges, especially if it meant getting top marks in her essay.

She had told one of the younger librarians she was taking

it out for her parents, who needed it urgently for a talk they were giving that week. The Young's reputation, and Drake's butter wouldn't melt smile, was enough to get the man to hand it over.

Well there had to be some advantages to having parents who had made the most important discovery of the 20th century, even if it was more than 20 years ago.

It was then Charles and Mary Young led an expedition to the rainforests of South America in search of the mythical city of El Dorado, the lost city of gold. But while there was no actual gold to speak of, the fame that came when they found it was like nothing the world of archaeology had ever seen before.

Even Carter locating the Tomb of Tutankhamun in Egypt was thought of minor importance compared to the Young's find.

If Drake, or her two brothers for that matter, had a penny for every time someone had come up to their family and asked their parents for their autograph, they could probably have afforded their own house to live in. Having one certainly would have made it easier to live under such an imposing shadow.

It was harder for her elder brother, Columbus, who for most of his life had desperately wanted to make his parents proud of him. But how do you go about doing that when they're the most famous explorers in the world?

Columbus' solution was to be constantly on the lookout for clues and leads that would take him on his own explorations and although there were plenty of adventures to be had, they were not in the same league as his parents. Well, not yet anyway.

But while Columbus was constantly seeking his parents' approval, Drake was trying to show Columbus she was more than just a stupid girl and that she too could lead an expedition, and maybe not get them all killed.

The previous year Columbus had taken them off on the

trail of the Golden Quail of Sir Peter de Quincy, an ancient medieval relic. It would have indeed made them front page news in Archaeology Today, had they managed to return it to Wellsbridge Museum. But they were not the only ones after the prize and their adversaries were a lot more ruthless than the Youngs, and they had guns.

If it hadn't been for Drake, the Golden Quail wasn't the only thing they wouldn't have returned with, they would have been without their baby brother Hudson as well.

Hudson wasn't exactly a baby but he still got into lots of bother. The one thing he was good at was building stuff. With the right tools and materials Hudson could pretty much build anything he set his mind to. For his eighth birthday he wanted a new train set and when his parents said no, he built one himself with its own station, extravagant points system, so that the trains could change lines, and even made a level crossing gate and bridge.

Drake had her talents, especially when it came to the brains department. She knew she was a lot smarter than her brothers in most things but when it came down to the explorations, Columbus always took the lead.

She had to agree he was a good leader, very brave, sometimes stupidly so, and most of all determined to succeed however bleak it looked for them.

It was only a matter of time before he too was on the front cover of Archaeology Today, it's just that Drake was quite looking forward to being on the cover with him, whenever that happened.

It was nice to dream but right now she had a school project to get finished and she was sure to get top marks with the information she was getting out of Kensie's.

She just had to make sure the librarians didn't catch her with it.

Chapter Three

Keeping Kensie's Historie of the Ancient British Tribes well hidden was going to be a bit more difficult now that the rowdy group of students keeping the librarians busy had left.

As Drake looked up from the slightly faded pages of the book she noticed one of the librarians walking towards her.

Her heart sank but then very quickly lifted when she noticed which librarian it was.

"Thank the gods of archaeology," Drake whispered. It was Madame Touquet, a very pleasant, and best of all, short-sighted librarian her mother was great friends with.

"I thought it was you," Madame Touquet declared rather loudly as she approached the desk Drake was sitting at.

"Hello Madame Touquet," Drake smiled as she carefully moved the book underneath the desk and on to her knees out of sight.

"You know Drake my lovely, it is so nice to see such a beautiful girl with her head in the books rather than in the clouds. There are so many silly girls these days. You won't become a silly girl, will you Drake?"

"I'll try not to," Drake replied a little awkwardly.

She didn't like deceiving Madame Touquet. With her neat, grey hair tied in the perfect bun, her tiny glasses perched precariously on the end of her nose and a pencil thin smile, she was a dear little thing.

Madame Touquet started to look a little puzzled. She was sure she had seen Drake reading a rather large, and interesting looking, book but now it was gone.

"But where is the book you were reading Drake my dear," she said.

Drake pretended to look a bit puzzled as well.

"What book, Madame Touquet?"

"Why the book you were reading just a few moments ago."

Madame Touquet was now starting to doubt whether she had seen Drake reading a book at all. It was true her eyesight was getting worse by the day and she knew full well it was because her glasses needed changing.

Madame Touquet may have been bright but she was also very nostalgic and her tiny glasses meant more to her than anything else in the world.

They were a gift from her father, whose one wish was for his only child to have the best start in life and go to university. As a French factory worker he earned little so he had to save up many months to buy the glasses. Such dedication inspired Madame Touquet to work very hard, so as not to disappoint her father, and she finally did get into university.

Unfortunately, the day before Madame Touquet's graduation, her father was taken ill and so couldn't make the trip over from France to see his beloved daughter receive her degree.

But even worse was to come for Madame Touquet as two weeks later he died. It was then she decided to always wear her glasses in memory of her father.

Drake knew this sad story well and so was safe in the knowledge she could convince Madame Touquet her eyes were in fact deceiving her and that there was no book.

She pointed to her pad and pen and explained what she was actually doing in the library.

"I'm writing a story about these three children who go on lots of adventures looking for treasure and this is the only place I can get some peace and quiet."

Madame Touquet looked disappointed.

"My dear you do have your head in the clouds," at which point she turned around slowly and wandered back to the librarian station gently shaking her head.

Poor Madame Touquet, Drake thought. She felt awful lying to her, especially as she really was reading a book for her studies. Drake was sure though that if Madame Touquet had caught her reading this book she would be even more disappointed with her.

When the old girl was finally out of sight Drake pulled the book back up on to the desk. A bit too keenly as it turned out because in the process of bringing it back up the back cover of the very old book got caught on a splinter of wood on the leg of the desk.

Oh no, Drake thought, she'd just broken one of the university's most important books. Her parents were definitely going to kill her for this.

She looked at the damage. It didn't look good. Drake certainly couldn't see a way of repairing it. The splinter had taken away a good slice of the top left hand side of the book and you could clearly see the back page through it.

Or was it the back page?

Drake looked closely at the page now peeping out from the top of the back cover. It appeared to have pictures on it. But Kensie's wasn't a picture book, it was just text.

She turned the cover over and looked at the last page of the book. She was right, there were no pictures.

Very strange, she thought. The page had to be a separate one tucked inside the leather-bound cover.

Intrigued, she turned the book back over again and gently

with the tips of her fingers tried to ease the piece of paper out from its hiding place.

Much to her annoyance the rip wasn't big enough.

Oh well, she said to herself. She'd ripped it already so making it a little bit bigger wasn't going to hurt that much.

She grimaced as she took her ruler and placed it carefully inside the opening she had made. Then, taking a quick look around the reading room to make sure nobody was in view, she moved the ruler slowly along the edge of the cover wincing as the metal tore into the leather.

Thankfully the old material didn't stand up to too much pressure and it wasn't long before the gap was wide enough to slip out the piece of paper.

Again Drake nervously looked around as she pulled it out. It turned out to be a folded document and, by the look of it, as old, if not older, than the book itself.

Unlike the pages it was a lot thicker and had a kind of waxy residue all over it.

Taking her time not to make any more tears in precious old documents, Drake placed it on the desk and unfolded it to reveal a swathe of bright blue and green colours - it was a map! And a very old one at that.

The blue was quite clearly a waterway of some kind, large enough to be a river, and the greenery had to be a forest or maybe woods. To one side there appeared to be a drawing of a settlement with mud huts and a fire but it was to the centre of the map that Drake's attention was immediately drawn. Standing out from everything else on the map was a huge green mound with brilliant streaks of bright yellow light shooting out from it.

Drake sat transfixed for a good few minutes staring and wondering what the light was until another group of students bustled into the reading room and broke her concentration.

In an uncomfortable mixed state of shock, excitement and nerves, Drake wondered what to do next.

This map looked very important, and it appeared to be

showing the location of some magical-looking place. If she was entirely honest with herself she knew she should tell someone about it, perhaps even her parents.

That would be no fun at all.

And then Drake thought of her older brother. Columbus would be so jealous if she found this place and then got on the front cover of Archaeology Today. Actually, Drake reckoned, just getting anywhere in the magazine before her brother would give her enough satisfaction.

She had started to hatch a plan the result of which, she had already decided, would be to go and find the magical mound, and become famous.

But first she needed to find out what area the map was showing. There were no place names she recognised and the only clues to where it might be were lines of text next to some of the more extravagantly painted landmarks.

One of Drake's many talents was ancient languages but she didn't recognise any of the words or place names.

She turned back to Kensie's to see if there were any clues or references to the map but just as she was about to start another group of students came into the room and, even worse, started making their way towards where she was sitting.

This place had too many students, she thought.

It was getting far too crowded for her liking so Drake took the map, folded it back up, and placed it in her coat pocket.

She then picked up the book and looked for a suitable hiding place.

The Wellsbridge college library was randomly scattered with lines of bookshelves so Drake headed for the ones closest to her.

They were lined with various books about the history of North America, which Drake thought was as good a place as any to hide a book about the ancient tribes of Britain.

Choosing two suitably older looking books with similar spines she snuck it in between them and noted the library reference code on the bottom of the shelf.

Keeping the number in her head she made her way back to her seat only to find a rather tall, spotty faced student clasping her coat in one hand.

She caught sight of the map precariously hanging out of the coat's right hand pocket and panicked.

"Hey," she yelled at the young lad, who spun around quickly with a startled look on his face.

"What are you doing with my coat."

With Drake's face turning a rather funny shade of purple the student was now starting to wish he hadn't bothered to find its owner.

"I thought you'd left it behind," he said nervously.

"Does it look as though it has been left behind. No it doesn't. So can I have it back please."

"Of course. Here you go," he said, handing back the coat very sheepishly. "Sorry."

"That's all right," Drake replied a little calmer now she had the map back in her possession.

The student then recognised her.

"Hang on a minute you're one of the Young children aren't you?"

"I might be," Drake sighed.

"Thought so. They're like my childhood heroes. You couldn't get me their autographs, could you?"

"No I couldn't."

Drake stared at him, picked up her things, and quickly left.

Her annoyance was short lived as she scampered out of the reading room and down the marble stairs to the library's huge timber framed doors.

Darting out into the open, she had to take a moment for her eyes to adjust to the brightness of the blazing sun. She had quite forgotten how long she had spent in the dark reading room and now, rubbing her eyes, she looked a lot like a prisoner who had just been released from a long stretch inside.

She stood for a while in the library quad squinting and

feeling the warmth of the sun's rays on her cheeks. It was a good day, in more ways than one.

She caught a glimpse of the stone statues that guarded the walls of the library. They were some of the world's greatest scholars, scientists and explorers.

Drake imagined them curiously looking down on her and whispering to each other.

"James," William Shakespeare turned to Captain Cook, "That girl looks as though she's found something pretty important."

"I think you might be right Bill. Could even be treasure," Captain Cook replied.

"Who knows what it might be," Drake said as she looked back down at her coat pocket and smiled.

"What I do know is that it's all mine."

Chapter Four

When Drake usually made her trips to and from the library she nearly always took a detour via Wellsbridge's beautiful Victorian park.

It was quite a bit out of her way but she didn't mind the extra trek just to wander past the ducks splashing about in the ornamental fountain and take in Mr Simpkins' incredible floral displays.

At that time the park keeper, who looked as though he was about as old as the park himself, had decorated his borders and beds a brilliant yellow thanks to the multitude of daffodil bulbs he had planted.

They looked glorious.

But although Drake knew she was missing out on another chance to look at the spectacle she took the direct route home that afternoon, along the town's busy High Street with people boisterously pushing past her in and out of the shops.

She wasn't a big fan of crowds at the best of times but with a valuable map in her pocket she felt even more uncomfortable. She just knew she had to get home quickly and this, unfortunately, was the best way to do it.

She needn't have worried as after a few minutes dodging the shoppers in the town centre she was at her turning for the suburbs. Within seconds she was back in among the side streets and avenues of Wellsbridge, all of which looked like a carbon copy of each other with their Edwardian three storey townhouses and great sprawling trees lining the pavements.

Shackleton Chase was no different and number 12 looked pretty much like every other house in the street.

It was a different story inside. The Young residence was a cross between a museum and a rubbish tip, not that any of the mess would have been regarded as rubbish to the family. Books lay strewn all over the place, as did various magazines and newspapers. What toys there were also lay in a similar state along with clothes, towels, rugs and blankets. There was plenty of storage space for all of this stuff but the Youngs didn't appear to have time to put anything in it, except the book cases, of which there were many, in the kitchen, the dining room, the study and the lounge, as well as most of the bedrooms and the attic. The disorganised state of the place aside, it still felt very homely.

There was a real fireplace in the front room always stacked full with whopping great big lumps of wood, which Drake's father eagerly looked forward to setting light to, and a mantelpiece over the top of the fire, dominated by a big picture of the family taken while on a recent holiday in France. Various archaeological nick-nacks adorned the shelves in most of the rooms and the walls were bursting with colour thanks to their mother's magnificent collection of landscapes, depicting mainly local rural scenes.

Drake delicately turned the key in the lock of the front door and opened it very slowly so she didn't get discovered. As she stepped inside, into the long hall, she could pretty much hear where the rest of her family were.

Hudson and Columbus were shouting at each other upstairs and her father was humming in the kitchen, from the sound of it, while frying something rather explosive.

That just left her mother. After a few moments trying to block out the humming and shouting, Drake's ears tracked her down to the study upstairs thanks to the sound of someone tapping away at the typewriter in there.

'Hooray the coast was clear,' she thought as she hung up her coat in the hall and took out the map from its pocket. Just as she did, her father popped his head around the kitchen door and spotted his daughter at the far end of the hall.

"Hello, had a good day?" he asked her cheerily.

Drake froze for a couple of seconds then answered. "Yes thank you father. I got a lot of work done on my project."

"Oh really, tell me more," he said before undoing his pinny, drying his hands on a tea towel, and then wandering out into the hall.

Drake panicked. "Won't dinner spoil?"

"No I've done all the hard work. It just needs to simmer now. Come on, tell me what you've been up to."

She knew she had to hide the map straight away so she jumped into the front room. That was one good thing about living in such a mess, there was always a good hiding place in the house. She quickly scanned the room and the first thing that struck her was Hudson's wooden train track.

'What was it doing in here,' she wondered. But there was no real time to ponder with her father walking down the long hallway so she popped it under the elaborate station her brother had built and then plonked herself on the sofa, picking up the nearest book she could find.

Within seconds her father was at the door.

"Hello."

Drake looked up from her book.

"Did you want me father?"

"I was just interested in what you got up to today," Professor Young said. And then he spied the book she was

18

reading. He looked perplexed.

"Drake, why are you reading Winnie the Pooh?"

She looked down at the pages and cursed her misfortune.

"I've been reading some pretty heavy stuff all day dad so I thought a little something light would make me a little more relaxed."

Drake was pretty pleased with her quick thinking and her father just smiled. His little girl was growing up fast but at least she still wore pigtails and liked Pooh Bear.

"I'll leave you to it gorgeous girl."

Drake smiled back, "Thanks dad."

When he was gone Drake waited a few seconds before putting down the book and getting up to go and retrieve the map from underneath the station, only for Hudson to come barging in.

Like his older brother and sister, Hudson had light brown wispy hair, except while Columbus had a neat side parting and his sister went for pigtails, Hudson's hair had a style all of its own.

If you were being kind you would call it spiky but a more accurate description would be messy.

It was the same with his clothes. Columbus and Drake were very neat and tidy in their attire but Hudson's preferred choice of clothing was scruffy shorts that came down to just below the knee and bright stripy T-shirts that were almost always dirty from grease, mud or food.

Given half a chance he would have worn the same clothes all the year round if his mother wasn't such a stickler for keeping him warm and clean.

That day he looked even messier than usual and was rushing around in a particularly excitable frenzy.

"Hi sis. What you been up to?"

"Nothing to concern you, Hudson."

Drake sighed. Now she had to get rid of her little brother, which was going to be a lot more difficult than her father.

"You haven't been at the library all day again?" Hudson

mocked. "Crikey Drake you might as well live there."

"At least I wouldn't be bothered by you all the time."

"You're going to end up looking like a book if you're not careful and then no one will ever want to kiss you."

"I don't want anyone to kiss me thank you very much. Now haven't you got anything better to do, like fall out of a high window."

Hudson stuck out his tongue. "Ha ha. Actually I'm doing some more work on my train set. I'm going to install a tannoy system to the station."

And then Hudson did something Drake was dreading he would do ever since he had walked into the front room, he looked down at the station. She shuddered. At first Hudson didn't notice anything and then suddenly, as though something had caught his attention from the corner of his eye, he bent down to take a closer look.

A cold rush of nerves raced through Drake's body as the inevitable slowly materialised in front of her. It was like watching a film that had been slowed down and Drake just sat there like a rabbit blinded by some headlights.

"Hello, what's this," Hudson said out loud as he lifted the station and pulled out the map from underneath it.

"Crikey it's a map."

Drake shook her head. The game was well and truly up.

"Of course it's a map, dunderhead. Give it here."

Hudson turned to his sister and asked where she got it from.

"Never you mind. Give it here."

"Not likely," Hudson replied with a twinkle in his eye Drake was more than familiar with.

"Hudson, give it here," she demanded.

Suddenly, their mother popped her head round the door. She had an annoying talent for creeping up on them without any warning, but Hudson was quick to spot her this time and managed to hide the map behind him without looking as suspicious as he usually did.

"What are you two arguing about?" she asked them.

"Nothing," they replied in unison.

Then their father shouted from the kitchen that dinner was ready and they both breathed a heavy sigh of relief.

"Right upstairs and wash your hands and faces."

"Crikey mum we're not that dirty," Hudson replied.

"Well I'm not," Drake added, smiling sarcastically at her brother.

Hudson poked his tongue out again and raced out of the room and straight up the stairs.

"Off you go Drake," her mother said as she motioned her to follow her little brother.

Drake knew exactly where Hudson was going, and it wasn't the bathroom. They may fight like cats and dogs at times but those blasted boys always stuck together.

She quickly followed Hudson upstairs and discovered her worst fears were realised as Columbus stepped out of his room with Hudson in tow waving the map in front of her face.

"We'll talk about this after dinner, won't we sis?"

"Doesn't look like I've got much choice."

"Not really seeing as we have the map now," Columbus said smugly. "And boy oh boy Drake does this look like one fantastic map."

"It's going to be different this time Col. Not like the other times where you get to make all the decisions. I want to be leader this time. I found it so I should be in charge."

But before Columbus could answer, their father shouted upstairs again. It wasn't wise to keep him waiting too long, especially when he had cooked the dinner. There was also the chance he might come and investigate so they agreed to finish their discussion after dinner.

Chapter Five

The brief break served them all well. It gave Columbus time to ponder all the questions that were suddenly buzzing inside his head, like where Drake had found the map, and what it would lead them to. It gave Drake plenty of time to rationally assess the situation. She knew a lot more than Columbus did and he was going to want to know everything. Of course, that would be no problem as long as he agreed to her conditions. Finally it gave Hudson an opportunity to eat lots of food, one of his favourite pastimes, and a chance to calm down from all the excitement. He was in no doubt they were about to embark on another adventure and he would need all the energy he could get. Food was sometimes scarce on their explorations, so he ate three helpings, which pleased his father greatly.

After dinner the three plodded back up to Columbus' room

and began planning what to do next.

Columbus looked very carefully at the map again and got the same thrill he had when Hudson first showed it to him.

"This looks pretty old," he said excitedly.

"You should have seen the book," Drake replied.

"What book?"

Columbus' enthusiasm was infectious. So much so Drake had quite forgotten her cunning plan not to tell him anything before he let her become the leader.

"The book I found the map in."

"Where is it?" Columbus asked her eagerly.

"Not telling," Drake said defiantly.

"Why am I even asking, it has to be in the library, you practically live there."

Hudson laughed. "That's what I said."

"Shut up you dunderhead," Drake snarled. "That's all very well Col but I've hidden the book and I'm not going to tell you where it is unless you let me be leader this time."

"Fine, you can be leader this time," Columbus replied.

'Crikey that was a bit easy,' thought Drake. Columbus had to be tricking her. Columbus saw the puzzled look on her face and smiled.

"Seriously Drake I think you're ready, and after all you did find the map. So leader what do we do now?"

Drake was well and truly taken off guard. She never thought in her wildest dreams Columbus would agree to it, and yet he had.

"Right, great, I'm leader," she said nervously wondering what they should do. "I know," she spoke out. "We need to go back to the library to have another look at the book."

"Good decision Drake," Columbus announced. "Let's go."

"Great let's go," Drake replied excited at her new position.

As Drake left Hudson pulled at Columbus' shirt.

"Are you sure about this Col?" he asked his older brother. "You're always the leader and I like you as the leader, you're not a girl."

"Of course I'm still the leader," Columbus reassured him. "I'm just letting Drake think she's the leader until we've got the book."

"See that's why you should be the leader, you're a lot cleverer than her."

"Thanks Hud."

"You're welcome Col."

At the library Drake led her brothers to the shelf where she had hidden Kensie's and they all took it back to one of the booths in the corner of the reading room.

Unfortunately the old room was pretty busy that evening and all three of them spent a few minutes nervously looking around them before Drake unfolded the map on the table.

They studied it for a while and then turned to the book. At first they couldn't find anything that related to it until Columbus turned to the pages about a tribe called the Cathwellas.

"There," Drake cried out, rather too loudly as a few people turned round and stared. "That's on the map," she continued in a whisper and she pointed to it on the parchment.

Sure enough it was there right above the words Marthica Regina.

"Regina. That means queen doesn't it. Queen Marthica must have been the leader of the Cathwella Tribe."

Hudson was still looking at the book.

"It says in here her name was Queen Martha," he said rather smugly.

"Martha, Marthica, that's close enough for me," Drake replied pretty excited by their discovery.

Just then another group of students wandered by and said hello to them.

Hudson quickly closed the book and Drake leaned over the map so they couldn't see it.

"This is ridiculous," Columbus said, frustrated by the disturbance. "We can't concentrate on something as important as this with all these people around. I suggest we take the book home."

"You must be joking," Drake said. "If we get caught with this book we'll be dead meat."

"But Drake every time we get the map out we're going to be looking over our shoulders all the time. We can only do this properly back at home in the attic."

She knew he was right. There were tons of pesky students buzzing all over the place and all it would take was for one of them to come over and discover what they up to and that would be that. Not the most brilliant start to her leadership.

"All right, give it here."

Drake took the book, marked the page they had been reading, and put it underneath her big jumper, folding her arms very tightly to keep it in place. Columbus folded the map back up and placed it in between his belt and his trousers, but underneath his blue blazer so no one could see it.

"Wouldn't it have been easy if we had brought a bag?" Hudson said.

"They check bags," Columbus replied wisely.

"Oh yeah. I forgot about that."

Drake shook her head again and walked out of the reading room very slowly indeed.

As they reached the top of the marble stairs Columbus spotted the last person they wanted to see that day.

"God it's Pinter."

"Where," Hudson replied.

"Down there, in the lobby."

As Drake spied him too, he looked up and spotted them all. The shock was clearly too much for Drake for as she went to walk down the stairs she missed her first step. Her foot slipped and as she went to steady herself on the huge wooden handrail, Kensie's Historie of the Ancient British Tribes slipped from underneath her jumper and fell down the stairs, landing at the bottom with a huge thump.

Unfortunately, it could not have ended up in a worse place, nestling at the feet of Professor Peter Pinter.

Chapter Six

To say Professor Pinter didn't like the Youngs would have been an understatement indeed.

Tall and thin with greasy short black hair, Professor Pinter insisted on wearing his robes at all times in college in order to make himself look a lot more distinguished, and older, than he actually was.

For many years he had worked tirelessly in the department of Archaeological Studies at Wellsbridge, hoping that one day he would finally become head of the faculty.

Finally, when it looked as though Professor Giles would never leave the college, out of the blue he caught a chill while on an archaeological dig in Sweden, and died.

Of course he did feel a little bit upset at his former boss' sad demise but when Professor Pinter heard the news he couldn't help a little skip in his step at the thought of his assured promotion to the top spot.

The very next day, the news reached England of the Young's incredible discovery in South America and from that point on his ambitions were doomed.

Wellsbridge insisted the married couple come and join their college, and as one of the most prestigious in the world they accepted at once.

Professor Pinter was distraught. He knew there was no way he could compete with the Youngs, now the world's most famous explorers and archaeologists. The only way would be to make a discovery more prestigious than theirs, and that was going to be a pretty tough task. But if Peter Pinter was anything, he was ambitious, and a little thing like trying to make the next most important discovery in the world wasn't going to put him off achieving his aims. It was out there somewhere, and he was going to find it, proving to the world he was the true archaeological explorer, not these fly by nights.

Of course, that was all before a certain little book fell at his feet and when he picked it up and realised what it was, he knew he might just have the right ammunition to finally get his own back on the Young family.

As he stood at the bottom of the staircase with the book in his hand he smiled the faintest of smiles as the three children bounded down towards him. As soon as they were at his side his face was one of pompous authority as though he was about to give them a right ticking off, which he was.

"Is it broken? Please tell me it's not broken," Drake asked him, very distressed by the whole affair.

"Thankfully for you it seems to be perfectly fine, which is a miracle considering its age," Professor Pinter replied quite sternly. "Do you realise how important this book is?"

The three children looked at him rather sheepishly.

"Of course you don't. If you did you wouldn't be throwing it down the stairs."

"I didn't throw it down the stairs. I would never do something like that," Drake protested.

"Well what are you three doing with it then?"

Columbus stepped in.

"I'm doing a history project and I kind of wanted to get a better mark than anyone else so I thought I would use a book nobody could get out and I told the librarian it was for my mother. It was wrong Professor I know, but please don't tell anyone. I've learned my lesson."

A likely story, thought Professor Pinter, especially as Columbus called him professor. He never called him professor, it was always Pinter, and it was always Pinter because he knew how much Professor Pinter hated it. It constantly annoyed him. He had worked damn hard to get his professorship so people should, at the very least, use it when addressing him.

"Well I don't really see how I can keep this to myself."

"You could always say you borrowed it," Columbus suggested.

"You're quick on your feet, aren't you boy."

Professor Pinter was impressed with Columbus but he was smarter, a lot smarter. He wasn't going to let anyone make a fool out of him, let alone the son of the Youngs. He thought a little and then made his decision. It was one that certainly surprised Columbus, Drake and Hudson.

"Right," Professor Pinter said. "I'll let you off this one time but I don't want to hear about any other important books going missing."

The children were stunned. They certainly weren't expecting Pinter to do that but they also weren't going to stick around so he could change his mind.

"Thank you professor," Columbus replied.

"Yes thank you very much," Drake added. "We are really sorry."

"Of course you are," Professor Pinter smiled at the girl.

When they had left he took the book back to the reading room with the strict intention of telling the senior librarian exactly what had happened and making a formal complaint about it.

That was before he noticed a tiny piece of scrap paper marking a particular page in the book. He opened it up and discovered it related to the Cathwella Tribe.

Now this was rather intriguing to Professor Pinter. Very little was known about the tribe except that like the Iceni tribe of East Anglia, who were led into revolt against the Romans by Queen Boudica, the Cathwella's most famous tribesman was a woman, Queen Martha.

Unfortunately for historians and archaeologists the only references to the tribe were in very old books like Kensie's. There was absolutely no other evidence that they actually existed, and certainly no traces of where they lived. Professor Pinter found it very hard to believe Columbus was studying them for school. Those kids were up to something. He wasn't exactly sure what, but it was definitely something, and it concerned the Cathwella Tribe, very interesting indeed, he thought.

Professor Pinter decided this needed following up, but how should he go about it. The Young children certainly weren't going to tell him what they were up to, so he was going to have to find out some other way. He decided to return the book but ask the librarians to tell him when it was taken out, and by who, just in case he needed it for his research again.

Those kids wanted that book, and the likelihood was they would try and take it out again. This time Professor Pinter would be watching their every move.

Chapter Seven

The rain lashed against the windows of the fifth storey of Senator House as Miles Orville looked out of his office laughing at the passers-by getting wet.

"Idiots," he shouted, although none of them could hear him through the thick glass. "Why haven't you got an umbrella or a mac, you fools. Look at you, you're soaked through, morons."

There was a knock at his door.

"What," he screeched.

His secretary popped her head round the door and asked whether he was all right.

"I'm just shouting at these idiots without their brollies, stupid limeys."

"Yes sir," she replied nervously and then quickly left before he started shouting at her.

Miles sat back in his huge chair behind his completely

empty desk and wondered what to do next. As a short, plump, rather brash American businessman he loved shouting at the British but if he was truly honest with himself, even that was getting boring now. He was in the business of making money but having already made a million pounds that week the thought of making more was also a bit dull. It was just all too easy.

He stood up again and decided to take a look at his loot. That always cheered him up. He switched on his intercom and told his secretary he wasn't to be disturbed for a few minutes before picking up a remote control and pressing a red button. An electronic whirring sound started up and a side panel in his office slowly swung open.

This revealed a small corridor leading to another door. Miles stepped inside and pressed another button, which then opened the second door. On the other side of it was a room probably like no other anywhere else in the world.

If you thought some of the world's greatest treasures were to be found in museums such as the Louvre in Paris and the Metropolitan in New York, think again.

On one side of the huge room the Mona Lisa stood next to the statue of David, while at the far end the Crown Jewels lay jumbled together on a side table. It was a treasure trove unlike anything else and nobody, apart from Miles, knew it was there. Looking around for something to do, he noticed Van Gogh's sunflowers were still lying on the floor. He picked it up to hang it on the wall and marvelled at its brushwork, before finding a place for it right next to the four original copies of the Magna Carta.

He then sat down at one of the many tables in the room and read through the American Declaration of Independence, chuckling to himself.

After a while he thought he better get back to his office. Someone was always after him and too much time in the 'Mine' room would start to make his employees suspicious, not that they would even dare become even slightly suspicious. People generally didn't mess with Miles Orville, it was bad for their health.

Back in his office Miles told his secretary he was ready to take calls now and within seconds the first one came through.

"It's Professor Pinter for you."

"What does that brainiac want?"

"I don't know sir, he wouldn't say, except that it was pretty important."

"Put him through then," Miles sighed.

"No sir, he's actually here, in reception."

"Heavens to Betsy," Miles exclaimed. "It must be important if he's left his beloved Wellsbridge. You'd better send him in Miss Johnson."

Professor Pinter quickly swept into the room and sat down in one of the two leather chairs that were situated opposite Miles.

"Hi Pinter, why don't you take a seat," Miles smiled. "What you got for me this time."

"I'm not exactly sure Miles but it could be the big one."

"What like the five other times you came into my office and said this is the big one, and what have I got to show for those, diddly squat, that's what."

"Come on Miles," Professor Pinter said slightly exasperated by his friend's comment. "What about that rare Moghul gold cross and the Rosary beads of Pope Gregory III," he said lowering his voice. "You know they should be in a museum and yet…"

Miles interrupted him.

"Yeah, yeah Pinter but really they're hardly the finds of the century. So what is this big one you're blithering on about."

"That's what I'm trying to tell you, this could be it," Professor Pinter told him excitedly. "Ever heard of the Cathwellas?"

"Friends of yours?"

"They were an ancient British tribe."

32

"My favourite kind of people, dead Britains," Miles smirked.

Ever since they met at St Cuthbert's boarding school more than 25 years ago, Miles had always been rather mean to the British, which is why he liked making their companies bankrupt.

There was their stupid game of cricket, "baseball, now that's a game," he would say, the way they talked "as though they had a golf ball in their gobs," and of course there was Mary Norman.

Mary was one of the prettier girls at the neighbouring St Mary's school. Because it was so close to St Cuthbert's, the girls and boys of each school often met on social occasions like concerts and dances, and it was on one of those very get-togethers, namely a tea dance, that Miles met Mary.

Her gorgeous long blonde hair, piercing blue eyes and her cute little smile were an instant hit with the young American and Miles fell in love with her straight away.

Unfortunately for Miles she didn't feel the same way and to make it worse Mary was a devious little thing.

She knew Miles liked her and she also knew he was rich so she did an unspeakable thing and pretended to like him, telling him how handsome he was and how much she loved his accent.

He lavished gifts on her and took her to the nicest places but after a couple of months Miles soon worked out she had been lying to him.

A boy he knew from his Latin class, a certain Peter Pinter, told him she had been seen kissing another boy.

Miles was devastated and for a good couple of weeks was a miserable wreck, and then something truly wonderful happened, Mary was expelled from her school.

No one was exactly sure what had happened, as Mary had always been a model pupil, destined for great things. Everyone thought Miles was behind it somehow but nobody could prove it. That was because he had in fact absolutely nothing to do with it at all, but he knew who had, his new best friend Peter Pinter.

To that day Miles still didn't know how he had managed it, he was just glad he had. He never trusted another British girl after that, and he wasn't too keen on the British men either, except Peter Pinter, who was kind of nerdy but determined and a little sneaky too, two qualities Miles admired.

That was pretty much why Miles was happy to help him out with his archaeological exploits, even when it did lead to some historical rubbish not even a museum would exhibit.

This one did sound interesting though, so Miles gave Professor Pinter the benefit of the doubt, yet again, and let him explain what was so damn special about the Cathwellas.

"Very little is known about the Cathwella tribe. In fact, I knew hardly anything about them until I came across a book I caught the Young children with the other day."

Miles sighed. "Not those little brats again, jeez I might have guessed they were behind it somehow."

"I know, I know, but if I hadn't caught them reading the book I wouldn't even be here."

"Those kids have definitely got a lot to answer for," Miles said quietly.

"Anyway," Professor Pinter continued. "They were looking up the Cathwella tribe, which is most definitely not something kids their age study these days, or in our day for that matter."

"Yeah, yeah what's so damn important about them," Miles said, getting a little frustrated.

"I'm getting to it. The Cathwellas are almost like a kind of fairy story. They were led by a fabulous queen called Martha, who had mystical powers."

"She was a witch?" Miles interrupted.

"Not quite. She was able to command the wind and the seas and the weather. She was supposed to be incredibly powerful and wise, and unbelievably wealthy. Other tribes tried to conquer them but they always failed, until that is

Queen Martha disappeared. She went on a quest to find a magical sword but never returned. The tribe, frightened that they would be attacked as soon as the surrounding tribes discovered what had happened, fled from their village and never returned."

There was a brief silence before Miles spoke out.

"That's it," he said, rather disappointed there wasn't a better ending to Professor Pinter's tale.

"Well it could be," Pinter replied mysteriously. "While researching them I came upon something else in a rather obscure journal which I thought would be right up your street.

"There are a few other tales about the tribe, mainly involving the people who tried to find her secret hoard of treasure, but there's also one about the sword itself, which is kind of another version of the King Arthur story."

Miles sat up intrigued. "I'm listening."

Professor Pinter smiled. He knew he had finally got Miles' attention.

"The magical sword Queen Martha went looking for was in fact the Excaliber, you know the one in Arthurian legend."

"Yeah I saw the film," Miles replied.

"Well the story goes she went to find the sword so she could use its magical powers to defeat a monster that was attacking her village. When she finally returned with it she discovered many of her tribes people had already been killed by the monster, so she set off immediately to find it and kill it. A few days later she returned exhausted and wounded, saying the monster was slain and the village was safe. But her battle with the beast cost Queen Martha dear and a few days later she was also dead. The remaining villagers took their queen, and the sword, and buried them in a secret burial chamber."

"And…" Miles was waiting for more.

"What do you mean 'and'. Excaliber, Queen Martha, what more do you want?"

"Are you trying to tell me this queen of the Cathwella tribe was the real King Arthur and that she is buried with the real Excaliber?"

"Interesting isn't it?"

"Far fetched is what it is."

Professor Pinter's smile was wiped from his face. Miles obviously needed a little more convincing.

"Miles, most of these wild goose chases, as you like to call them, are speculation, but as you keep on telling me you have to speculate to accumulate. What if the Young children are on to something, and what if they've found some evidence of the Cathwella tribe, and what if the myth about Queen Martha and Excaliber is true."

"That's a lot of what ifs."

"I know but do you really want to miss out on the opportunity?" Miles sat and thought for a few seconds while Professor Pinter looked at him intently, willing him to agree to help him out.

"All right you got me, I'm in," Miles suddenly said.

He was right. Miles didn't want to miss out on this opportunity however far fetched it might be. They said there was no El Dorado until the Youngs discovered it and if their kids had half the skill, and luck, that their parents had, he would be a fool not to follow it up.

Despite knowing full well Pinter wasn't up to the job, he told the professor to go back to Wellsbridge and keep a close eye on what those kids were up to. He had someone else in mind for that job and after Professor Pinter had left his next call was to him.

"Hello it's me, I've got another job for you. I'll be in touch with the details in due course but just to warn you there are some kids involved in this one."

There was a brief silence while Miles listened to the man's answer. "I didn't think it would bother you. Good. This one could be very important indeed, and I don't want anyone getting in my way."

Chapter Eight

"Well what does this section say then?" Columbus sighed.

"I don't know," Drake replied getting angrier by the minute. "I keep on telling you it's like nothing I have ever seen before."

The really annoying thing for Drake was that it looked familiar. There were some words she recognised from Latin and Greek but then there were all these others that made no sense at all. Quite clearly some were place names but there were also a number of sections of text which seemed to be describing something else. Columbus had suggested they might be directions to the treasure, or whatever the map was leading to, but Drake couldn't be sure.

What she did know was the boys were being very unhelpful by getting so frustrated with her, especially Columbus. To be fair she was supposed to be the expert in languages but Drake felt even she shouldn't be expected to know some obscure ancient British dialect.

These Cathwella people were certainly a weird lot, why couldn't they speak Latin or Greek like everyone else, or even Celtic for that matter.

She studied the map for the umpteenth time that week and rubbed her eyes.

"You getting tired Drake?" Columbus asked.

Drake mistook his sympathy for mocking. "No, I can go on all night," she protested, sitting up straight and picking up the map with even more determination.

"You could go at this all week and still not find any answers. Look Drake I reckon even a history professor would have trouble deciphering this lot, don't worry about it."

"We need that book," Hudson interrupted.

All of them knew he was right but they also knew how risky it was going back to get it. Pinter may have let them off the hook the last time but heavens knows what he had told the librarians, and if they were caught for a second time it would most definitely be curtains for them.

And yet without the book the treasure trail stopped there. Despite Drake's best efforts they were going nowhere and no amount of extra research was going to help them. For the last four days they had practically exhausted their parents' library, as well as their own, and had very little to show for it. They were certainly no closer to finding the starting point for their next exploration.

"I'm sure there was some kind of index at the back of the book with some funny looking words," Hudson continued. "Perhaps it will help us work out what it says."

"Are you sure?" Drake asked him. "We only looked at the book for a matter of seconds, how could you possibly know there was an index in it?"

"Drake," Columbus interrupted. "There doesn't appear to be any other option. I know you're the leader but I think we should go back and try to smuggle it out again."

Columbus knew being a Young meant the prospect of

adventure always outweighed the prospect of getting caught so it was no surprise to him, or anyone for that matter, when Drake agreed.

Back at the library, the two boys waited in the lobby while Drake went up to the main reading room and the librarian's desk. Fortunately, the same young librarian who let her have the book the first time around was on duty. She gave him the same speech about her parents needing the book urgently and once again he obliged. He was just about to hand over the book when one of the more senior librarians turned up at the desk and asked him what he was doing. He tried to explain who Drake was and that it was normal practice to lend out these kinds of books to her but the older librarian wasn't having any of it. Kensie's was far too important to be taken out by anyone, and that also meant the Youngs. All through this exchange of words Drake kept quiet. She didn't want to upset the older man but at the same time she felt a little bit guilty at having got the younger one into trouble. She was just about to say something when the young librarian asked to speak to his boss 'out the back.'

"Will you excuse us for a second," the young man said to Drake as he led the other librarian into a back room.

Drake must have only be waiting a matter of minutes before they both returned all smiles and both more than willing to let her have the book.

She did think it rather odd that the older man had changed his mind so easily but there was only really one thing on her mind and that was to get her hands back on that book.

The older man handed over Kensie's with a broad smile and apologised. Drake returned the smile and walked off back down the stairs to meet her brothers.

"Nice one sis," Columbus congratulated her. "I don't know how you do it but I'm sure glad you did. Right let's get back home."

Chapter Nine

The three made their way back to Shackleton Chase as fast
as you can with a huge, priceless 16th century book under
your arm and as soon as they got inside they sprinted up the
stairs to beneath the attic door.

While Columbus reached around his parents' door to get
the stair hook for the attic steps, Hudson went into his room
to get a chair. Placing it underneath the hinged ceiling door
above his head, he got up on to the chair and stretching
upwards, pushed it open with a flick of his wrist.

As usual it swung downwards and missed Hudson's face
by inches.

Drake shook her head. "One of these days that door is
going to knock you out, you loon," she told him.

Hudson just smiled and asked Columbus to pass up the
stair hook. Once in his hand he skilfully directed the metal

rod to underneath the steps and lifted them down with one great big swoop, again narrowly missing his head.

"Hudson!!" Drake called out.

"Don't have a stress sis," Hudson coolly replied. "I haven't been hit yet."

As Hudson got down from the chair his brother and sister climbed the attic steps up into the roof space.

Like most of the Young's house it too was full of books, scattered all over the place along with various clutter their parents had accumulated over the years from their many expeditions. There were African tribal fighting masks, rugs from Persia and even a small South American pigmy's canoe all scattered about the floor, and all of it gathering dust.

In one corner of the attic Columbus had managed to persuade his parents to set aside a little den for the children. It was sectioned off with a rickety wooden petition behind which there was a wooden table, which their father had sawn the legs off so they could sit underneath it.

Around the table there were a number of assorted shelves, all different in shape, and mostly stacked with books, magazines and maps apart from Hudson's little shelf, which had a selection of old flower pots brimming with various tools, nails and screws.

Drake got the map out from its hiding place, which was underneath the rather colourful rug that the table sat on, and placed it on the table.

Columbus, who had been holding the book, turned to the back pages and discovered the index of words that Hudson had said was there.

"Told you," he said rather smugly.

Drake then began the long process of taking the words from the map and deciphering them using the words in the book, which she then wrote down on a piece of paper. At first Columbus and Hudson watched her working away trying to get a hint of what it all meant but after a while Hudson got bored.

"Anyone else thirsty?" he asked the others.

"How can you think of drinking at a time like this," Columbus replied.

Hudson shrugged his shoulders and clambered back down the steps and then the stairs to the kitchen where he poured himself a glass of squash.

Drake was finally starting to get somewhere with the map.

"There's something about a sword," she told Columbus.

"What sword, whose sword?"

"I don't know yet, I assume Queen Martha's. It says here it's a magic sword."

Columbus could hardly contain himself. "A magic sword. Fantastic, this is going to be the find of the century," he declared.

Drake continued studying the map as Hudson climbed back up the stairs with the glass of squash in his hand.

"How are we getting on?" he asked them but before they could answer Hudson tripped over one of the many books lying on the floor and fell to the ground. In a fairly dramatic fall his glass of squash went flying sending the once thirst quenching drink all over the place.

"You ruddy idiot," Drake scolded him before she turned back to the map and noticed it was soaked with the squash.

"The map," she gasped.

"Don't panic Drake," Columbus calmed her. "We'll just wipe it down. It should be fine."

He got his handkerchief and started to dab the centre of the map only to find some of the green paint was coming off.

Drake saw it immediately. "Columbus stop," she called out but it was too late as the green mound had almost disappeared.

"Wait a min," Columbus said as he studied the area a little closer. Underneath where the green mound once was there now appeared to be something else. He took his handkerchief once again and started to clear away some more of the green paint to reveal a brilliant golden sword. Where the bright yellow shafts of light had looked as though they were coming out from the mound, they now surrounded the sword.

"What about that then," Columbus said in awe of what he had just discovered. "I think I've found your sword Drake."

For the next few seconds they starred at it, all very excited about what had just happened then Drake told Columbus not to start dabbing anywhere else. Now that they had found the prize the last thing they wanted to do was destroy the directions to its location.

After a few more minutes Drake had all but translated the text on the map and she explained to the other two what the map was.

"It's showing the final journey of the great Queen Martha of the Cathwella tribe.

"Look," and she pointed to the map. "This is the trail the men and women of the village took and the mound is where she was buried along with her sword."

"Yes but where is it?" Columbus asked her.

"I don't know," Drake said with some disappointment. "The place names aren't in the book and they don't look familiar at all."

"Why don't we ask dad?" Hudson suddenly said.

"Are you crazy," Columbus replied.

"Well why not. He knows loads of stuff like this."

Drake pondered what her little brother had just suggested and reckoned it wasn't quite as awful as Columbus obviously thought.

"Actually," she said. "That isn't half bad. We could just ask him about one of the names on the map and that would give us enough to find the sword."

She looked at the map again and picked out the largest town close to the Cathwella's village.

"Here look at this place, Camolod," she showed her brothers on the map. "If dad knew what this place is called today we could roughly work out where the village is in relation to this river. From the site it should be easy to locate the trail the villagers went on to get to the mound."

"Yes but what do we tell dad when he asks us why we want to know about this place called Camolod?"

"We just send Hudson along and he can tell him he saw it in a book."

"He'll never believe that," Columbus replied.

"Hey," Hudson protested.

"Well he won't Hud, will he?"

Drake thought for a while and then came up with a plan. She gave Hudson his instructions and he and Columbus smiled at its brilliance.

Hudson then set off downstairs, picking up some items from his bedroom before seeking out his dad. While he did this, Drake and Columbus waited up in the attic for their little brother to return. They desperately wanted to see how well he carried out Drake's plan but they knew if they all went along, their father would definitely know they were up to something.

Chapter Ten

Hudson quickly found his dad in the living room reading his newspaper and with a small pot of paint and paintbrush in one hand and a block of wood in another he sat next to him.

"Hello Hudson," his father said looking up from his paper.

"Hello dad," was all Hudson said before opening up the tin of black paint on the arm of the sofa and then dipping his brush in.

"Hudson, what are you doing?"

"I'm painting the name of my station," Hudson replied in all innocence.

"Well can you do it on the table," his father told him.

"Sorry dad," Hudson replied as he picked up his materials and went over to a small table in the corner of the room.

"Hudson, please put some paper down before starting."

"Of course dad," and Hudson got off his chair and came back to the side of the sofa where there was a pile of old newspapers on the floor.

He picked a few up and asked his dad whether he was allowed to use them. His father nodded and went back to reading his paper. So far Hudson had done his best to get his father's attention with not much luck so he decided to improvise and wrote the name of the station on the block of wood before spilling some of the paint on the table.

"Whoops," he called out loudly.

His father had heard that phrase far too many times before

and with a certain amount of dread asked his youngest son what he had done.

"I've spilt a bit of paint on the table," Hudson confessed nervously.

Professor Young knew a bit of paint was always going to be a lot of paint when Hudson was concerned and so got up off the sofa and went over to the table.

As he peered over Hudson's shoulder he was pleasantly surprised to find the little bit of paint was in fact just a little bit and all captured by the extensive amount of newspaper Hudson had strewn across the table.

Then he noticed the name of the station.

"Why have you called it Camolod?" he asked his son.

"Pardon dad," Hudson replied.

"Camolod, what gave you the idea to call your station Camolod?"

"I heard one of the professors say it the other day."

"Which professor?" his father asked him.

"Oh I don't know they all look alike to me. Why is it an important place?"

Then Hudson noticed a familiar glint in his father's eye. It was an expression which usually spelt trouble, for it meant his father was about to drone on about a fascinating historical fact. It just so happened this was a historical fact Hudson was dying to hear.

"Well Camolod is actually a very interesting place," his father began. "It is one of the old names for the ancient Roman town of Colchester in East Anglia. You see very often Roman place names dropped their endings after the Romans had left them, like Londinium, which became London. Well the Roman name for Colchester was Camolodunum. Drop the unum and you get Camolod. Now the really interesting thing about this is that some people have said Camolod was the real Camelot, you know the legendary home of King Arthur and the Knights of the Round Table, but of course no proof has ever been found to support this theory and many people now believe the West Country was a more likely place."

Now that Hudson had done all the hard work he wanted the final piece of the puzzle, so he asked his father where Colchester was.

"In East Anglia like I said. Actually you know exactly where it is, your Uncle Robin and Aunt Julia live near there."

"Great, thanks dad."

Hudson's work was complete but his father hadn't finished with him quite yet. Professor Young had been pondering, as only professors can. The name Camolod had begun a thought process in his head, which was now whizzing around his brain at a million miles a second. Questions were popping up here, there and everywhere and he needed a few answers.

"Hudson," he said. "Are you sure the professor said Camolod?"

"I think so."

"Are you sure it wasn't Camelot?"

Hudson may have been the youngest of his siblings but he still had a suitable number of years behind him to realise what was happening. He knew if he wasn't quick on his toes his dad would be asking all kinds of difficult questions, which his brother and sister would definitely not want him to answer.

"You know dad. It might have been Camelot," he replied, hoping to put his dad's newly found interest in what they were doing, finally to bed.

"I just thought it sounded like Camolod."

"Yes that must be it," his father said to himself. "I wonder though."

Then, as his father often did when he had something on his mind, he walked off in a kind of befuddled daze before bumping into his wife in the hall way.

"Ah Mary. Do you know anyone in the faculty who is

working on a project that might involve Colchester?" he said.

"No, why do you ask?" she answered a little perplexed by his question.

"Well Hudson heard a professor talking about Camolod."

"Are you sure?"

Hudson sighed, now his mother was intrigued.

If there was one thing worse than a pondering professor it was two professors pondering together.

"Well he thinks he did but he told me he didn't know which professor it was. Apparently we all look alike."

They both smiled.

Hudson wasn't smiling. While all of this was going on he had been standing at the living room door getting more and more uncomfortable as the conversation progressed. Why did his parents have to be so darn inquisitive all the time? Why couldn't they be like normal parents and not pay attention to a single word they said? The plan was starting to go very wrong and Hudson knew he had to do something else to make them both drop it.

"Dad," he started. "If Colchester is where the Knights of the Round Table lived then is the Holy Grail somewhere in Essex."

Mary looked at her husband disapprovingly.

"Charles, what have you been telling the children?"

Hudson's father tried to defend himself but his youngest son had done the trick and dropped him right in it.

"I only mentioned the Camolod myth because he thought he had heard someone say it."

"Well clearly he's heard someone talking about Camelot. Dr Evans is working on the myths of Camelot, it must have been him."

She turned to Hudson and described Dr Evans and Hudson duly obliged nodding and stating that it sounded just like the man he had heard talking about Camolod.

"You see Charles. Stop filling the children's heads with

silly ideas."

And off they both went still discussing what Hudson may, or may not have heard.

Hudson saw his chance to make a break for it and sprinted upstairs to rejoin the other two, who were almost nearly out of their minds after the long wait.

Hudson explained what had happened and then gave them the answer they had long been waiting for.

Columbus patted his little brother on the back and Drake gave him a peck on the cheek.

"Well done little brother," she said. "You're smarter than you look."

"You were the one with the plan."

"Yeah, yeah, are we all finished with this self appreciation society," Columbus interrupted. "If you two had quite forgotten we have to start preparing for our next expedition and I reckon it's going to be our best yet."

Chapter Eleven

The Youngs had quite a bit of time to prepare for the trip as it was a good few weeks until their Easter holidays. But all of them made sure they used that time well. For a start they didn't utter a word of it to their parents. Hudson had told them how his father had got interested at the slightest mention of the word Camolod, so any more discussions about Camolod, Queen Martha, the Cathwellas or Colchester were strictly off limits even if they thought their parents were out of earshot – it was too risky.

Then there was working out where they had to go. As soon as they had found out Camolod was Colchester, Columbus was able to plot a course from the Essex town right up to where the old Cathwella village used to be. From there it was just a case of using a compass and following the detailed landmarks on the map. Of course after all these years some have them may have disappeared but Columbus still believed he would be able to find it.

The only remaining thing to do was come up with a convincing argument to persuade their parents to let them go and see their aunt and uncle in Essex for a week. Ordinarily this would have been easy but for their Easter holidays this year their parents had planned a trip to Norfolk to take part in a dig on the Blickling estate. It would be good fun, they always were, but hunting down a magical sword would be better. It was just a case of getting their parents to agree to it.

Once again Drake was the girl with the plan.

Uncle Robin was a fisherman and what he didn't know about fish wasn't worth knowing.

Columbus was doing a project at school about fish and fishing, and what a great way of getting a good mark for it than by talking to real life fishermen. In fact he would probably ace the project if he actually went out on a fishing trip with his uncle. That would give him a good mark for his biology paper, making it more likely he would get good enough grades to get him into a very good college.

"Do I get any say in this?" Columbus scowled. "You know I hate boats and I'm not doing a project on fish or fishing for biology."

"Little details," Drake replied. "You probably will at some stage and anyway it appeals to mother's desire for us to do well at school."

"Doesn't she think Uncle Robin is a bad influence on us," Hudson added.

"Ah I thought of that as well. We ask her at dinner when both mum and dad are there and when she says no, I'll just say it's because she thinks Uncle Robin is a bad influence. She'll deny it because she won't want to insult dad's brother in front of dad and then dad will get all uptight because he knows mum is insulting his brother and then there'll be a discussion the result of which will be dad saying to mum well if she doesn't think Uncle Robin is a bad influence then why doesn't she let us go and mum will have to say yes because if she says no then dad will know it is because she thinks he is a bad influence on us."

Drake stopped to take a breath as Hudson and Columbus looked at her in a rather bemused state of wonder.

"Well, what do you think?" she asked her brothers.

"Well, for a start I can't believe you said all of that in one breath," Columbus told her. "And secondly you're a genius. I still don't like the boat thing. Can't Hudson do it?"

"Not likely," Hudson replied. "Everyone knows I'm rubbish at biology."

So it was decided and at dinner that evening the three children played out Drake's plan to perfection.

Charles and Mary Young went to bed in a terrible mood that evening but on the plus side their children went off to sleep safe in the knowledge that their Easter holidays would be spent with mad Uncle Robin and searching for treasure.

It wasn't long before the day arrived and after packing their rucksacks they said goodbye to their parents. Their mother or father would have normally taken them to Wellsbridge station but they were doing some rather heavy duty packing of their own in preparation for their dig so they got a taxi to drive them there.

At the grand old Victorian station Columbus paid the driver, and was in such a jolly mood he gave him a nice big tip. Then along with his brother and sister they gathered up their packs and made their way to the ticket desk.

Their train journey that day would take them via London and Columbus wanted to be sure which line on the underground they needed to take to get to Liverpool Street station so he asked the man at the ticket counter.

He was a grumpy old fellow and told them it was the Circle Line or the 'yellow one that goes round and round.' Columbus replied cheekily that as rule that was what circles did but the man just sneered and gave them their tickets.

"What platform does the next train for London go from," Drake then asked the man.

"You're so blinking clever why don't you find out for yourselves," he told them all very moodily and then pulled down the black blind with a bright red 'position closed' sign on it.

Columbus spotted a sign with several destinations on it

which eventually ended in London which then at the side had an arrow pointing to platform 1.

"Come on," he said pointing to it. "It's over there."

As they got to the top of the steps that led over the bridge to platform 1 Hudson saw a long bright red train waiting for them. At the side of one of the carriage doors there was a young guard fiddling with a green flag and looking across the large station area for any stray passengers. As soon as he saw the Youngs puffing their way onto the platform he called over.

"Are you lot wanting the Northern Flyer for London," he shouted.

Columbus called back that they were.

"Well get a ruddy move, on it's about to leave."

The three immediately picked up their feet and sprinted over to the carriage door where the guard helped them on board.

"Crikey, you lot look like you're about to go on some adventure," the guard smiled at them.

"We are," Drake smiled back.

When on the train they found a little carriage to themselves, put their rucksacks on the luggage racks and settled in for the long journey to London.

Hudson had brought a pack of cards and they all played gin rummy to pass the time until he had won Columbus and Drake's pocket money for the next five weeks and then they played the cow game. Drake spotted the most with 65.

It wasn't too long before the fields and woodland of the countryside were replaced with the lines of houses and factories that told them they were now travelling through the suburbs of London.

All of them had been to London before, many times in fact, but there still was nothing like it, especially arriving by train. The grotty outskirts of their country's great capital always provided them a great thrill. It meant they would soon be wandering around the hustle and bustle of the great city, along busy streets and across picturesque parks, through marvellous museums full of treasures and in and out of brightly lit shops full of wonderful things to buy.

That day the anticipation was not for the city itself but for the fact it would be their stopping off point to another place they hoped would also fill them with wonder and surprise.

At the station they got off and excitedly made their way to the underground only to find it was rush hour and the whole of the city appeared to be packed on to the platforms. They tried to make their way to the front with no luck and after getting stabbed once too often by the ends of numerous commuters' umbrellas, Hudson decided enough was enough and collapsed on the floor.

Columbus and Drake rushed to his aid but as they arrived he gave them a little wink and yowled in pain.

A kindly old man in a pinstripe suit, who just happened to be standing nearby, asked them what the problem was.

Drake didn't like it but she knew what to do. Her brother had pulled this stunt a few times before.

"I'm afraid he needs his medication," Drake told him as mournfully as she could. "If he doesn't get it soon it may be too late."

Immediately sympathetic to their cause the man then grabbed two other similarly suited men and told them they must get this young lad to a doctor straight away.

A doctor was the last thing they needed so Columbus stepped in.

"Our mother is waiting for us at Liverpool Street," he told the men. "She has his tablets."

It was all the information they needed. They picked Hudson up and while Columbus held on to his pack they made their way through the crowds informing everyone about the emergency. Within seconds they were all on the tube train and in a few minutes at Liverpool Street station.

Drake thanked the men and gave them all a kiss while Columbus told them they could manage from there. He certainly didn't want them coming up to the railway station to discover their mother wasn't actually around. Thankfully Hudson had managed to regain enough strength to walk and with a little help from his brother and sister they all carefully stepped off the tube and wandered slowly along the platform towards the escalators. As the train sped off they waved farewell to the men on the train who returned the wave through the window. As soon as it was down the tunnel and out of sight Hudson stood up straight and smiled.

"That saved us a bit of time."

Columbus threw his rucksack back at him. "Well seeing as you've made a miraculous recovery you can have that back for a start."

Drake wasn't too impressed either. "I still think it's a pretty mean trick Hud."

Hudson couldn't believe what he was hearing. "Are you kidding?" he said dumbfounded. "We get past the crowds. We got a seat on the tube and those guys think they've done their good deed for the day. Everyone's a winner, especially us. Anyway I don't know about you two but I'm getting hungry and the sooner we get to Colchester the sooner we get some of Aunt Julia's homemade biscuits."

Columbus smiled. "Come on then biscuit boy let's see how long we have to wait for the next train out of here."

Chapter Twelve

Thankfully it wasn't long and soon they found themselves rocketing past lush green Essex meadows, meandering rivers and streams and big thickets of trees.

By the time they finally pulled into Colchester station it was starting to get dark. They collected their rucksacks and wearily stepped off the train to find their larger than life uncle waiting for them on the platform.

A mountain of a man, Uncle Robin always stood out from the crowd. Compared to his older brother, Charles was a lanky beanpole but while as tall as him, Uncle Robin was also round, very much like a slightly deflated beach ball. It was not just his size that was striking. He had a swirl of curly white hair and a weathered face only a North Sea fisherman could wear with pride. He was also well-known for his broad smile, which was nearly always emblazoned across his face, and with the arrival of his favourite niece and nephews it was wider than ever.

"Why if it isn't the Young explorers," he bellowed out to them.

"Uncle Robin," Drake replied. "Are we glad to see you."

"Especially Hudson," Columbus added. "I think he's about to faint any minute now if he doesn't get one of Aunt Julia's chocolate cherry biscuits."

Uncle Robin laughed. "He's in luck I have some in the van. Good job too, we'll have to wait a while before we can get onto the island as the tide is up."

Robin and Julia Young lived in a gorgeous little fisherman's cottage on Mersea Island, about ten miles south of Colchester.

Surrounded by river estuaries and tributaries the only way onto Mersea was across the Strood causeway, which every now and then flooded with the incoming tide.

You would expect a fisherman like Robin Young, who knew the waters around Mersea like the back of his hand, not to get caught out by the high tides, but he often did. Of course the fact that getting stuck on the mainland also enabled him to stop off at his favourite pub, situated conveniently next to the Strood, had absolutely nothing to do with it.

That evening, as was his normal custom while he waited for the waters to drop, he parked his van in the gravelled car park of the Sozzled Sailor and took his niece and nephews inside.

Popping his head around the door into the smoke-filled bar he asked the landlord whether it was all right to bring in the kids. As one of the pub's most frequent visitors the answer was always going to be yes. Uncle Robin led them through the main bar jam packed with an assortment of burly-looking bearded men some of which were smoking pipes, all of whom had a pint glass of frothy brown liquid in their hands.

As they walked past the various tables and chairs dotted

around the cramped bar, most of the men said hello to Uncle Robin and asked him how he was. One of them even patted Drake on the head and told Uncle Robin she was a right little beauty and couldn't believe she was related to him.

"Brainy too," Uncle Robin said proudly. "Mind, you know how their dad is."

Eventually they made it to a tiny room at the back of the pub that joined the main bar and was away from the smoke and chatter. Uncle Robin sat them down on a rickety wooden bench and asked them what they wanted to drink.

"Pint of beer please uncle," Hudson brazenly asked him.

"Squash it is then," he announced and headed off back to the bar.

As much as they loved their uncle, their mother was right, he was a bad influence on them. The only other time the three had ever been in a pub was also when they were with Uncle Robin, and Columbus remembered it being a pretty grimy one at that.

He soon returned with a jug full of orange squash and a pint of almost pitch black beer.

He took a big gulp, sighed and sat back in his chair.

"So what brings you hoodlums down to this neck of the woods then," he asked them out right.

"Well we wanted to come and spend some time with you and Aunty Julia," Columbus answered him.

"And sprats can talk. I'm not as stupid as you think and as much as you lot love my wife's cooking and my tall tales I reckon you're down here for some other reason and we're not leaving this pub until you tell me what it is."

All of them looked at each other aghast. Uncle Robin always had a canny knack of knowing exactly what was going on but to have figured it out this quickly caught the Youngs well and truly off guard.

Columbus looked at Drake to come up with an answer while Drake did the same to Columbus. Hudson knew it was a safe bet nobody expected him to talk, so he quietly got on

58

with the task of drinking his squash and finishing off the chocolate cherry biscuit his uncle had given him in the van.

"Well, cat got your tongues," Uncle Robin grinned, knowing he was right.

"Fine we're off on a little adventure," Drake offered an explanation.

"Drake," Columbus protested.

"Oh don't you worry your little heads. I won't tell your parents," Uncle Robin assured them. "I just want to make sure you're not getting yourselves into any trouble."

Convinced by this, and the fact they could tell Aunt Julia he had taken them to the pub, Drake gave him an edited version of why they were there.

"There's supposed to be an ancient tribal village near here which no one has ever found."

"And you think you know where this village might be," Uncle Robin interrupted her.

He shook his head and smiled. "You lot are so like your father it's frightening. He was always going off on some grand expedition when we were young boys. Never found anything mind, still he's made up for that since then, hasn't he. Where is this tribal what you call it?"

"It's just outside Colchester near a small town called Wivenhoe."

As soon as Columbus had uttered the name of the place, Uncle Robin's face dropped.

"I might have guessed it would have been Wivenhoe," he sighed.

"I take it that's not a good thing," Columbus said.

"That's an understatement," Uncle Robin started. "The place maybe called Wivenhoe now but years ago it was known as Wyvernhoe."

"Dragon's hill," Drake said with a sudden sense of realisation. "I hadn't thought of it before. A Wyvern is a kind of dragon and hoe is the Saxon word for hill or high ground. It can't be true though Uncle Robin, there isn't really a dragon

59

there?"

"Well I would have agreed with you when I was your age," Uncle Robin said sombrely. "You see there is a path that runs along the river and it used to be very popular with swimmers, especially a group of boys from the village. Now for years there had been stories about some kind of serpent or dragon inhabiting the waters around Wivenhoe but they, like me, thought they were just that, stories. One bright sunny day these boys wandered off down the riverside path to their favourite spot. I think there was a particularly large tree there that overhung the water. As usual all four of them jumped from the tree into the water, except that day only two came out. Both boys were excellent swimmers but neither body was ever found.

"But that's not the end of it. A few years later a Wivenhoe fisherman, who had a few too many whiskies, fell overboard on his way back into port. One of his shipmates dived in after him but he had completely disappeared from sight. Everyone thought he had drowned and his body had been swept away downstream but days later his right leg was found washed up on nearby Whitehouse Beach. It had huge teeth marks right through it. Experts were called in but to this day no one has been able to identify what it was that took a bite out of him."

Uncle Robin paused, leant over the table and finally whispered, "the really frightening thing about it is the place where he had fallen in was almost the exact spot where those boys went missing."

When Uncle Robin had finished his gory tale he sat straight back up in his chair and took another gulp of beer.

The children didn't quite know what to say. He was well known for his stories but with the manner in which he had told the last one, they all knew he was deadly serious.

Uncle Robin then smiled. "But that's not going to stop you, is it?"

Drake breathed a sigh of relief. "God, Uncle Robin, I really thought you were serious this time."

"Oh mark my words Drake, everything I have just told you is the gospel truth and if I was you I'd steer well clear of the place but if you're anything like your father I'm betting the lure of this village will be just too much. If you keep your wits about you I reckon you'll be all right but a word of warning, stay out of the water."

"Don't worry Unc," Hudson said. "I think you can take it as read we'll be avoiding any kind of water, especially after the little story you just told us."

"And you're not going to stop us?" Columbus asked.

"I couldn't stop your father going off on his little jaunts, so what hope have I got with the three of you," Uncle Robin chuckled. "Now come on, your Aunt will be wondering where we have got to and of course it hasn't been the pub, all right?"

"All right," they replied in unison.

Chapter Thirteen

It was a particularly warm day in the city of London but that didn't bother Miles Orville. He was lounging in the back of his air-conditioned limo as it drove along the busy streets of London towards his favourite cafe.

He had already got his secretary to phone on ahead to book the entire place out for lunch and it was with a gratifying smile that Miles arrived outside Henri's to discover a small group of people trying to get a peek at the famous celebrity inside.

Of course none of them had a clue who he was but when he stepped from the car and sauntered inside past the hushed whispers from the crowd he lapped up the attention.

His lunch companion for that day had arrived by a much more secretive entrance via a back alleyway, through some cellar doors before finally being seated in a secluded booth at the back.

"Is he here?" Miles asked one of the waitresses. The waitress nodded. "Good, I'll have the rack of ribs and a beer and my friend will have the soup and a cup of Earl Grey tea, no milk, no sugar and make it strong."

"Yes sir," she answered nervously and made her way back into the kitchen.

Once she was gone the place was deserted. Everyone at Henri's knew Miles was not to be disturbed. Even Henri himself, who was a good friend of the businessman, kept himself and his staff behind the closed doors of the kitchen and waited for his call.

The café was a rather jolly little place with pictures of famous French people on the wall and red, white and blue streamers hanging from the ceiling. Despite its size there were about 20 round tables crammed inside, all of which had the French flag draped over them as tablecloths.

Miles liked the place because he liked the French, and he liked the French because they hated the British almost as much as he did.

He wasn't too keen on the cooking though but having made friends with Henri and his chef, Michel, his money had persuaded them to cook him whatever he wanted.

On any normal Friday lunchtime Henri's would have been packed out but every once in a while the call came through from Miles' office to close the place up. It was a pain shutting up shop and drawing the blinds so no one could see inside but Henri didn't mind as Miles made sure he was well compensated for the inconvenience.

Empty, apart from the two diners, certainly made the normally very lively city café very eerie indeed but Miles liked it that way. His friend didn't.

"Why all this cloak and dagger?" the man said in his thick Eastern European accent.

"I don't want people seeing us together, do you?"

The man pointed to the noise of the people milling about outside the café. "So why make a fuss," he said gruffly. "They all think you some kind of famous person."

Miles smiled. "I know. I think that's rather funny, don't you?"

"No," the man said firmly.

Most would have been pretty scared of the man sitting opposite Miles Orville and those who knew him well enough were petrified of him.

At nearly 7ft tall and almost 20 stone Dimitri Kozkov was a man not to be messed with. With curly black hair and deep-set eyes, he was certainly no gentle giant and there were plenty of people who had crossed his path who could testify to that. There were a great deal more who could no longer testify to that precisely due to the vicious nature of the man.

He had fled his home country of Poland several years ago after a fight in a bar, which resulted in the death of a very influential man. He eventually ended up in London where his physical appearance and his fighting skills soon drew him to the attention of some of Britain's most notorious criminals, one of which recommended him to Miles. For the last five years he had been working for the businessman, sorting out problems whenever they arose. The Pole, as he was known in criminal circles, had a particular knack at solving them and Miles was more than willing to pay for the privilege.

This time it wasn't so much a problem, more of a situation Miles wanted him to oversee. A few hours previously Miles had got a call from another of his contacts who had been ordered to follow the Youngs.

The phone call was to say they were in a town called Colchester.

"What you want me to do, kill them?"

Miles grinned. "No. Well not yet anyway."

"What do you want me to do then?"

"These little brats are currently hunting down a great treasure, perhaps the greatest treasure I will ever get my hands on. I do not want that treasure to fall into their hands or anyone else's for that matter."

"What is this treasure?"

"Dimitri, all you need to know is that it is very valuable and I want it. I need you to get to Colchester as soon as you can and hook up with Professor Pinter."

"Not that idiot."

"That idiot happens to be a friend of mine and he knows a lot more about this stuff than either you or I. Mind you that wouldn't be too difficult in your case."

The Pole grunted disapprovingly at the last comment. Miles often insulted him. One day it would be an insult too far but while the money kept coming he let them pass.

Miles continued. "Report back to me as soon as you get there and tell me what they are up to."

The Pole nodded and then Miles called out to the kitchen for their lunch.

After they had eaten The Pole left the café by the same way he had gone in and Miles went back out the front, smiled at the people still waiting outside, and got into his limo.

Back at his office he immediately got on the phone and called up Professor Pinter.

"Peter dear boy, what do you know about Colchester?"

There was a pause on the other end of the line before Professor Pinter answered.

"Colchester?"

"Yep that's where those Young kids headed for after they took that book out again."

"How do you know about the book?" Professor Pinter said a little surprised.

"Come on, this is me you're talking to, I have eyes and ears everywhere, including the Wellsbridge library. They told you when the kids had taken the book out again, then they told me. I've had them followed ever since."

"And now they're in Colchester?"

"That's what I said," Miles replied.

There was another pause before Professor Pinter answered

again.

"Well that's odd," Professor Pinter thought out loud.

Very odd indeed. Nobody really knew where the Cathwellas came from but East Anglia was the last place Professor Pinter thought it might be. Perhaps it was because he had got caught up in the King Arthur myth and Excaliber that he had assumed the tribe would be from the West Country but thinking about it why not East Anglia. And why not Colchester. When the Romans invaded in AD43 they made it their capital and when they left it remained an important trading post.

Then it dawned on him.

"Of course, Colchester," he said. "Colchester used to be called Camolodunum during the Roman times but when they left I think it then become known as Camolod."

"And your point is?" Miles asked.

"Come on Miles, surely even you can work this one out. Camolod sounds a bit like Camelot."

"You're kidding me."

"Well why not. In fact I'm amazed there hasn't been a paper on this."

"Hey," Miles interrupted. "Before you get any ideas of making a name for yourself, you find me that sword. I've sent The Pole down there already and I want you on the next train to meet him."

Professor Pinter winced. "Not that thug, really Miles I can handle this one on my own."

"Not likely Peter. I don't want any foul-ups on this one. If the sword is there, I want it."

Professor Pinter disliked The Pole. He was a brute and worse than that, a stupid brute. He knew nothing about archaeological treasures or their value. All he was interested in was the money. As a highly thought of professor at one of the world's most esteemed universities, Professor Pinter had a reputation to maintain and getting involved in The Pole's criminal activities was not the right way to go about it.

Their last trip together had nearly cost him a spell in prison and it was only thanks to Miles bribing an ambassador that he got let off the hook.

After that little incident he had vowed never to work with him again but Professor Pinter knew how highly Miles regarded The Pole. He also knew how much Miles wanted that sword, so it was with a great deal of anxiety that he agreed. He told Miles it would take him an evening to pack his things but that he would be in Colchester by the next day.

"Don't worry," Miles assured him. "The Pole won't step out of line this time. He is under strict instructions."

What those instructions actually were Miles wouldn't say and that was what really worried Professor Pinter.

Chapter Fourteen

Columbus woke to a beautiful sunrise and Hudson snoring. As they came up over the estuary waters, the brilliant sun-rays streamed through the flowery curtains into his bedroom and right on to his face. As he was stirring in his bed Columbus heard the faint creak of the front door shutting behind someone.

As inquisitive as always he threw off the covers and jumped from his bed to find out who it was. At the window he pulled back the curtain just enough to see his uncle in his thick woollen jersey and waders waddling down the path that led from the cottage towards the quayside.

Columbus had quite forgotten how early fishermen had to get up but it didn't seem to bother Uncle Robin who was whistling a very merry tune as he went on his way.

Columbus settled back into bed and although Hudson's train-like snores prevented him from falling into a deep sleep, he dozed, dreaming about the adventure that lay ahead.

It was the smell of bacon that next coaxed him from his bed but that was only after Hudson had smelt it first and sprinted to the bathroom to get washed and dressed. Aunt Julia's breakfasts were almost as legendary as her dinners and Hudson couldn't wait to re-acquaint himself with them.

Columbus was the next downstairs, followed soon after by a yawning Drake.

"Did you sleep well dear?" Aunt Julia asked her.

Drake smiled and nodded her head.

Aunt Julia laughed. "It's the sea air you know, always wipes you townies out. Now come and sit down and have some breakfast."

And what a feast it was. Anyone would have thought Aunt Julia was feeding a small army with the amount of food that was laid out on the kitchen table. There was a mountain of crispy bacon piled high on a plate, a huge saucepan of scrambled eggs, plenty of sausages sliding about in a bowl and several racks of toast. If her two brothers hadn't already waded in to it, Drake wouldn't have known where to start.

"Oh I forgot the tomatoes," Aunt Julia suddenly said.

"Really aunty," Columbus muttered while munching on some bacon. "This is just great."

Aunt Julia had always been a bit of a perfectionist and like her food her appearance was properly done. Her long grey hair was tied up in a neat bun and she wore a checked apron, which was pulled tight around her tiny waist in a smart bow. Her small frame was pretty surprising bearing in mind the food she regularly dished up, but one look at Uncle Robin and you could guess where most of it went. That morning it was Hudson, Drake and Columbus who scoffed the lot, giving them more than a perfect start to their expedition.

After gorging themselves they rested for a while chatting with Aunt Julia about life on the island before they finally made their excuses and went upstairs to pack their rucksacks.

Aunt Julia followed them up and was surprised to find out

they were off somewhere.

Wandering into Drake's room to find her packing was rather disappointing for Aunt Julia. "Oh, I thought we would go sightseeing in Colchester today," she said.

"Sorry Aunty," Drake replied. "Columbus has this plan to go and visit the remains of a Saxon village. Well I say remains I think it's just a few mounds of grass."

"Well why don't I come with you," she said eagerly. It wasn't often she saw her niece and nephews and although she wasn't very keen on visiting historically significant bits of grass, she was willing to join in with their fun if it meant spending some quality time with them.

Of course that was the last thing Drake and her brothers wanted.

"Columbus really had his heart set on a little expedition," Drake explained. "You see we're going to camp out overnight and come back tomorrow."

"And your parents know about this?" Aunt Julia said a little astonished. "What am I saying, of course your parents know about this. I'm sure they positively encourage you to do it."

Aunt Julia knew she was of a different generation to Drake's parents but she still held strong opinions about the way children should be brought up and it wasn't remotely consistent with Charles and Mary's cavalier approach to it.

Drake tried to reassure her. "Oh we camp out and go on trips all the time. Columbus and I know what we are doing."

"I'm sure you do dear but there are some rather nasty people out there, and some pretty ghastly places. I just want you to be careful."

"It will be on a proper camp site," she lied. "And we'll give you a call when we get there, so you know we're all right."

"I know you think I'm an old worry head but ..."

Drake interrupted her. "Don't be silly aunty. You're only looking out for us and I think that's sweet."

"So do I," said a voice from the doorway. It was Columbus who was already packed and raring to go. "Come on sis, we don't want to miss our bus."

"Don't be silly, I'll give you a lift," Aunt Julia insisted.

"Actually aunty I was rather looking forward to the trip on the bus," Columbus said feeling a little awkward about upsetting her.

She smiled. She was disappointed but it was their hols and she didn't want to be the mean old aunt who made a nuisance of herself.

"Well all right then, but if you lot think I'm letting you go without a good packed lunch to keep you going, you're very much mistaken. I don't care if you miss the bus, there'll be another one along in 45 minutes and I would have finished it by then. Now go and play in the garden while I make it."

'45 minutes,' thought Columbus. 'How big was this lunch going to be?'

"Really aunty," Columbus said out loud. "It's fine, and anyway we've got enough to carry already."

After listening to the conversation that was taking place on the landing Hudson decided it was time he offered his opinion on the matter. He stepped out from his room and told Columbus he was talking nonsense.

"Of course we can carry it. It would be a crime not to."

And that was that. The three children carried their rucksacks down to the front hall and then popped out for a stroll along the quayside while Aunt Julia busied herself in the kitchen.

On their return there was a rather large holdall sat next to their rucksacks and after saying their goodbyes Hudson found himself carrying it.

"You wanted the blasted thing," Columbus told him as soon as they were out of earshot from their aunt.

It was rather heavy but he knew it would be worth all the effort in the end.

Fortunately for Hudson it wasn't far to the bus stop and

when their bus finally got into Colchester it took them straight to the train station.

A brief walk to the ticket desk, and then the platform, and Hudson was able to put down the bag again while they waited for their train.

The trains to Wivenhoe were few and far between but when it finally did arrive the children got a very pleasant surprise as the brown carriages were pulled along by an old bright red steam engine.

"Fantastic," Hudson exclaimed and went off to speak to the driver.

Columbus and Drake carried their luggage onto the train and found a quiet compartment for them to sit in.

A few minutes later an excitable Hudson joined them and just as he was about to begin telling them about the technical aspects of the train, Columbus stopped him in his tracks.

"Right you two we need to keep our eyes peeled for this path. It leads from Wivenhoe to the site of the ancient village. According to the ordnance survey map it goes past the station and winds its way back between the river and the train track."

Columbus got the crisp new map out from the front of his rucksack and unfolded it on his lap.

"There do you see," he pointed at the dotted red line that ran alongside the river. "We should be able to see it from the train as we get into Wivenhoe. In fact we should be able to see the site of the old village. The old Kensie map says it is here," and he pointed to a small square that marked out an area of wide-open space fairly close to the train track.

"Here are the woods right next to it and somewhere in there guys is Queen Martha's sword."

"They're not very big woods," Hudson remarked.

"Your point being?" Columbus replied.

"Well you would think after all these years if this sword is in these small woods someone would have found it by now."

"Well they probably would have done if they hadn't all

been scared off by this myth about a dragon," Drake said. "I bet the Cathwellas made up the story to stop grave robbers raiding Queen Martha's tomb."

"What about those boys?" Hudson asked her.

"There's no such things as dragons Hud," she chuckled. "Those poor boys just got caught out by the tides."

"Yeah but ..."

"Hudson!" Columbus was starting to get annoyed with his younger brother. "There's no such thing as dragons. It's just a silly story. Now come on we need to look out for this path."

Hudson wasn't happy about it but he kept quiet anyway.

As the train slowly shunted out of the station he took up his position with the other two by the window. As the engine gathered pace they were soon out of Colchester and into the countryside. Within minutes the River Colne appeared from nowhere by their side.

"There's the river," Columbus said excitedly as he turned to the map to see where they were. "We must be about here. Not far now."

Past some docks, the train continued to chug along the track towards Wivenhoe and the further they went the wider the river got.

"We must be really close now," Columbus said, and just as he did the furrowed fields they had been whizzing past on their left suddenly gave way to an open piece of land surrounded by large trees.

"There it is," he declared before quickly racing out of the train compartment into the corridor to peer out of the opposite window. "And there's the path."

Sure enough there it was, a narrow path that crossed the train track at the entrance to the large grassy field, and then wound its way back along the riverbank to the village of Wivenhoe.

"Seems a shame we can't jump out here really," Hudson thought out loud.

"The walk will do you good," Drake replied.

Soon after, the train began to slow and the long platforms of Wivenhoe station came into sight. The Youngs leapt from their seats and grabbed their bags as the guard yelled out the name of the station.

"Wivenhoe, Wivenhoe station."

"Come on you lot this is where the fun really gets started," Columbus told them.

Chapter Fifteen

As one of the prettier fishing villages in the county, Wivenhoe often got visitors.

They paid a trip to the place either to enjoy afternoon tea on the quay or a walk along the estuary towards Alresford Creek. Sometimes they went even further over the footbridge to Brightlingsea.

After clambering off the train at Wivenhoe Station those visitors would climb the wrought iron bridge to the other side and walk through the gate, turning left towards the quay and the fishing cottages.

Very few people turned right out of the gate, because that just took them back along the railway line towards Colchester, and if they wanted to do that they could simply take the train.

Once outside the station entrance, turning right was exactly what Columbus, Drake and Hudson did, and they immediately started looking for the path that would lead them to the site of the ancient Cathwella village.

"It should be over there," Columbus said, pointing to a large number of prickly looking bushes and hordes of nettles.

"Let's ask someone," Drake suggested.

She went back inside the station office and asked the man behind the ticket desk, who was slightly taken aback by her question.

"Why on earth do you want to walk there?" he asked suspiciously.

"My brothers and I fancied a stroll along the river."

"There's a much better walk the other way you know, past the quay."

"Yes we know but we wanted to take the less beaten track."

The man laughed. "You'll be lucky if you find the track, let alone take it. Mind if you really want to go that way your best bet is to go to the end of the car park and wade through the nettles by the brick wall."

Seeing Drake was in shorts he reckoned that would put them off, so he was quite surprised when Drake thanked him and went back outside.

As it happened the man's advice was very good, and after Columbus had picked up a rather large stick and beaten a way through the nettles where the man had told them to go, he discovered a narrow gravely path leading off into the distance.

By the look of it the path was very rarely used and in places was overgrown with brambles but Columbus could see further on where the path appeared to widen out and was easily passable.

"Come on you lot, I've found it."

Columbus beat the nettles back even further to make a little corridor through which his brother and sister sidled past the stingers.

On the path all three suddenly became very aware they

were finally on their trip and as well as being a bit nervous, there was definitely an air of excitement around.

Columbus led from the front with his OS map and Drake followed on with the Kensie's map.

So as not to damage it she had put the map in a plastic bag and every now and again she called out to Columbus where they were to go.

Of course Columbus knew exactly where to go, having studied the two maps in great detail beforehand, but he knew Drake was still under the impression she was leader, so he nodded at her instructions to keep her happy.

Hudson dawdled along behind the two looking at the surrounding scenery. It really was beautiful. To their left the river meandered to and fro up the estuary with grassy marshland and mudflats standing between them and the water. At various intervals a small copse of trees would spring up along the path and then some banks of reeds, swaying in the river breeze and teaming with twittering birds. The other side of the path, and across from the railway line, there was the imposing sight of Wivenhoe Woods, staring at them from behind the track as though ready to pounce on them at any moment. Hudson didn't like looking at the huge number of trees all crammed together like they were waiting for a rush hour train. He was kind of scared of them, especially after what Uncle Robin had said. If there was something nasty lurking about these parts, it couldn't have chosen a more menacing place than the dense woodland.

As Hudson was taking in the sights the other two began arguing up in front of him. They had come across a path to their right, which went under the railway line and into the woods.

Columbus had suggested they take the path, and with the use of his compass, they could bypass the village and go straight to the burial site.

Drake on the other hand insisted they stick to the riverside path and get to the village. Kensie's map was the only thing they had which showed a clearly defined route through the woods to the site where Queen Martha was supposedly buried. The only thing was that route started from the old Cathwella village.

"We're wasting time Drake," Columbus told her. "I've looked at both of these maps and I reckon I can get us there, no problem."

Drake knew Columbus was good with maps, and his sense of direction would put a migrating swallow to shame, but once inside the woods there were no features they could follow. The Kensie's map gave precise directions and even had landmarks, neither of which Columbus' trusty OS map and compass had.

"I'm sorry Col, I think it's too risky."

"I don't know about you Col but I would quite like to see this village," Hudson interrupted.

"There's probably not a lot to see," Columbus said.

"Yeah but since we've come all this way it would be a shame to miss it."

Columbus smiled at his little brother. He realised he was getting carried away with himself and so agreed with the other two to carry on along the path.

"Anyway," Hudson said, as he looked down the path, which ran under the dark, dank railway bridge, "I don't much fancy going down there."

The three carried on, Hudson particularly happy to be walking out in the open, and it wasn't too long before the river, on one of its sweeping meanders, crept up on them from behind.

Just past a tiny path, this time to their left, Drake caught sight of it through a small line of trees and within yards it joined them all, virtually lapping at their feet.

Columbus could see exactly why young boys would want to jump in it and have a swim. It was very inviting to suddenly see the glistening water in all its glory as the trees stepped aside to reveal its wide expanse. With the sun going in and out of the clouds, like it was playing a game of peek-a-boo with the blue patches of sky, the river sometimes took on a shadowy ominous shape. That all changed when the bright rays finally did fall onto the water making it look like it was filled with a million glistening diamonds all dancing about the ripples.

All three marvelled at the sight for a while until Drake's eye was caught by something else gleaming from the water. Long and silvery green, at first she thought it might be just a piece of driftwood floating along the river, but on closer inspection it appeared to be something a lot more intricate, with distinctive jagged edges.

Her eyes were immediately transfixed on the object and as it bobbed away from the shore Drake followed it almost robotically. Without a word to her brothers she walked up the path keeping an eye on it. Eventually she got to a group of trees that had partly fallen into the river, as though some of the branches had felt the need to lean over to take a sip of the water.

Keeping her eyes on the river she climbed out onto the trunk of one and across a large branch to get a closer look, but as she made her way along the tree the object floated that little bit further away, making it impossible for her to see exactly what it was.

'Just a little bit further,' she thought to herself.

She edged a few more inches and then all of a sudden a cracking sound shook the tree from the trunk to the very branch she was clinging to. Within seconds the huge wooden bough was sent crashing into the river below with Drake holding tightly on to it.

Both Columbus and Hudson heard the gut wrenching noise and turned to see their sister plunge into the water.

"Drake!" Columbus shouted as he ran over ran to the river's edge.

All of a sudden Drake's head popped up from the surface and she took a gasp of air. She waved at her brothers who looked very relieved to see her.

"Sorry," she called out to them. "I thought I saw something."

"Just get back here will you," Columbus replied.

As Drake started to swim the few metres back to the path she felt something grab her ankle and she went under for the second time.

For Hudson and Columbus this was even more shocking than seeing their sister fall from the tree and as the river swallowed her up they screamed at the top of their voices.

Columbus instinctively waded into the water and started swimming out to the area where she had disappeared.

"Col, the monster," Hudson called out to him.

"For crying out loud Hudson get in here and look for Drake," Columbus shouted back angrily from the water.

Hudson nervously jumped in as well but almost as soon as he did a huge fountain-load of water surged up in front of them both. The wave sent a huge wall of water splashing over their heads which stopped them dead in their tracks.

As they coughed the salty water from their mouths and wiped their eyes they were about to continue their search when they saw Drake spluttering by the side of them.

Both grabbed hold of her so tightly she winced. She didn't mind. Like her brothers she wasn't keen on going under for a third, and maybe, final time.

Slowly they made their way back to the path where they pulled themselves up on to the bank.

After a few moments getting their breath back Columbus asked her what had happened.

"I don't know. Something grabbed hold of my ankle and pulled me under."

"What was it?" Hudson said nervously.

"I told you I don't know. It felt like a huge weed or rope but it was pulling me back towards the shore and then I felt something a bit slimy on my face and then it let go and I was pushed up by this torrent of water."

"The monster." Hudson said quietly.

"Shut up Hudson," Columbus told him.

"Look I know you guys don't believe in this kind of stuff but you tell me what else that could have been."

"Weeds, the current, any number of things," Columbus said. "The main thing is you're fine, we're all fine. Now no more about it."

They did what he said although both Hudson and Drake looked at each other with the same thought in their heads. That was no clump of weeds or a sudden surge in the tides. That was the Wivenhoe monster and they were definitely not going any where near the water again.

Chapter Sixteen

Fortunately going near the river was not going to be a problem as a few yards up the path it swept away from them for the final time to be replaced by marshes and even some stretches of grass.

On one particular piece of grass the three decided to stop and eat the lunch Aunt Julia had packed for them. It was also a good opportunity to dry their soaking clothes on some nearby bushes. Sitting in just their underwear, they then tucked into the grub. It was well up to Aunt Julia's standards and after they had wolfed down the vast majority of it, leaving some sandwiches for supper, they lay back and rested a while.

They knew a lot more lay in wait for them and that they should really get going and find the village site but behind them the path went up a small incline and into a dark stretch of woods. After the frightening experience they had just encountered all of them wanted a little break from danger although none of them would admit it to each other.

Across the river they could see the cranes of Colchester docks in the distance and closer a field full of grazing cows. It was a very calming rural scene so they sat and chatted about all kinds of stuff like what birds they could see along the river and whether huge tankers ever came up that far.

After a good few minutes Columbus knew they were just delaying the inevitable and so decided to get things back on track.

"We must get on. The clothes should be dry by now."

He got up from the grass and checked his shirt with the palm of his hand. Sure enough it was bone dry. He put his trousers back on while Hudson and Drake put on their shorts and all of them reluctantly continued their journey.

Up the path and into the woods, they were suddenly shielded from every piece of surrounding countryside as branches and brambles slowly engulfed their way. It was a long corridor of greenery and at some points the three had to duck their heads to get past.

Thankfully they soon came out into the open and Hudson was actually pleased to see the woods over the railway line. Within seconds, though, the path took them back into even more sinister territory as the bushes crowded around the path and plunged them in to darkness.

"Crikey O'Reilly," Columbus broke the tension. "This is worse than the last one."

"Come on let's jog a bit so we can get out of it," Drake said.

But before they could set off a mournful groan bellowed from up above their heads. As the noise got louder and louder it seemed to be coming from all around but with the thick woods all about them they could see nothing.

"I don't like this," Hudson said. "Let's peg it."

For once all of them agreed and they sprinted from the place as fast as they could. As soon as they did the groaning stopped and even more pleasing than that Columbus spotted a stile by the side of the railway line. He breathed a huge sigh of relief. If that was the stile he thought it was then by climbing over it and crossing the railway line they would finally be in the field where the ancient site of the Cathwella village once stood.

He told the others and with a new found spring in their step they marched to the stile and saw a very agreeable sight.

Stretching uphill in front of them was a huge lush green field with huge trees dotted all around it. In the middle was some scrubland and to their right was the edge of Wivenhoe Woods. Just across the scrubland to their left Drake could just make out a circle of trees that looked very similar to an area on the Kensie's map.

"You know what," she declared very proudly. "I think we've found our village."

She held up the map within the plastic bag for the others to see and sure enough the circle of trees was there, sitting gloriously in one corner of the faded parchment.

"Race you to it," Columbus said smiling.

"Hold up you two," Hudson said. "There's a train coming."

Columbus and Drake looked down the line. They couldn't see any train.

"Where?" Drake asked him, a little puzzled by her little brother's warning.

"Wait a tick you'll see."

Sure enough just as Hudson had uttered those words a faint puff of smoke suddenly appeared over some tree tops in the distance. Then they heard the unmistakable chuffing of a steam train and within a few minutes the next Colchester train was pounding down the track.

"How did you know there was a train coming?" Columbus asked him.

Hudson looked at his watch. "Because there's one due about now," he replied.

Drake smiled. "Let's give the passengers a wave," she said cheekily. "They won't be expecting anyone round here."

"God they'll think we're the Railway Children," Columbus added.

"Come on stop being a stick in the mud."

So they took off their rucksacks and climbed the stile ready to wave at the train. As it got closer the driver slowed down, as was the regulations for approaching a crossing, and as the red steam engine trundled past, Hudson and Drake feverishly began to wave while Columbus shook his hand in a rather uninterested way.

Through the windows some of the people on the train looked visibly shocked to see them waving at them. Others smiled and waved back but towards the end of the train the Youngs were in for a surprise themselves. There, sitting bolt upright and starring out of one of the windows was the very familiar face of Professor Pinter. Surveying the surrounding area for any signs of archaeological interest, he caught sight of them immediately. To be fair the children did rather stick out like sore thumbs on top of the stile waving away like crazed loons. Of course as soon as they saw Professor Pinter their hands, as well as their faces, dropped.

As the train carried on the professor followed them with his eyes with a horrible, smirking grin on his face. He couldn't believe his luck. His informant at Colchester station had told him the children had caught a train to Wivenhoe that day but to find out their exact location so quickly certainly made him very happy indeed. He noted their position and told his accomplices there was no need to go searching the village for the Youngs. He knew exactly where they were.

"I don't believe it," Columbus said. "Can anything else go wrong today?"

Then it started to rain.

At first it was a brief drizzle, which sent the Youngs scurrying to the nearest tree, but as it got heavier, and the clouds became even more dark and sinister, they put on their macks and trudged up the hill towards the ring of trees.

"I told you there'd be nothing here," Columbus said despondently.

Drake pointed out that the circle of trees were there and that if there had been something a lot more obvious, they wouldn't have been the first to discover it.

This cheered him up a little bit.

"There's a little mound here," Hudson pointed out.

Columbus walked over to where he was standing and pointed out the rabbit poo that was littered all around it.

"I think that might be a rabbit warren Hudson."

He knew Hudson was only trying to help but he still felt a little cheated. If only there was something to absolutely prove it was the Cathwella village.

"Come on Columbus," Drake said. "Stop moping about. This really is an amazing thing. Just think a thousand years ago the Cathwella tribe were here getting wet just like us."

He laughed.

"You know we could always start our own dig," Drake continued, "but I don't think we've really got the time, do you?"

"You're right, especially with Pinter on our tail. Look Drake, if you don't mind can I make a few suggestions."

Drake nodded. "Go right ahead."

"Thanks. Right the first thing we need to do is find shelter from this rain. It looks like we could be in for a real storm and I want to be out of the open anyway in case Pinter and his goons decide to pay us a visit. They know we're here but they still don't know why, or what our final destination is."

Even Drake had to admit when they were up against it Columbus was a pretty good leader. He had made mistakes in the past but she was tired, wet and horribly confused about why Professor Pinter was following them and how he had managed to do it.

Columbus knew they had to hide and he picked the perfect place, just behind the circle in a secluded crop of trees. He ushered Hudson off to get some wood to make a shelter and then, with Drake, cleared the floor of twigs and branches before putting up their tent. Rather than light a fire he told them all to take off their wet clothes and put on every single piece of dry clothing they had with them. Fortunately the temperature wasn't that cold so once inside their tent, and with the rest of Aunt Julia's packed lunch inside them, they were very comfortable indeed.

"Why do you think Professor Pinter is following us?" Hudson asked his older brother.

"I suspect he's looking for the same thing we are," Columbus replied.

"Yes but how does he know what we're looking for?"

"Kensie's," Drake suddenly called out. "When he took it off of us in the library he must have had a quick look himself. Perhaps there was another map or some information in there we didn't spot."

"He may have just reckoned we were on to something with the book and then had us followed," Columbus added. "Whatever happened he's here now and almost certainly hoping he can take all the glory for our find.

"Right we are going to have to keep a look out tonight. I'll go first, Hudson you're second, Drake last. Is that all right with everyone?"

They nodded.

"Good, let's try and get us much sleep as we can. We are really going to need our wits about us now."

Chapter Seventeen

"Well done Hudson," the driver called out amidst the smoke and huge noisy chuffs the big red engine was belching out. "We are making fantastic time. I can't believe you've never driven an engine before. You're a complete natural."

Hudson peered through the steam and wiped the sweat off his forehead. The furnace was incredibly hot but he didn't mind as the trees and fields raced by and the wind swept through his hair.

"Hudson, Hudson."

"Yes I'm doing it, I'm doing it."

"For god's sake Hudson."

"Stop pushing me I'm doing it."

"Come on lazy head it's your turn."

Hudson finally opened his eyes to see his brother crouching over him prodding his sleeping bag with a stick.

"Ouch, that hurts," he protested, still half asleep. "I was having a brilliant dream you know."

"Yes well I would quite like to have a sleep myself, so get up."

Hudson grumpily climbed out of his sleeping bag and put on his coat.

A drenched Columbus told him straight away the rain was still pelting down and the lashing the roof of the tent was getting confirmed it.

He sighed heavily and asked Columbus what he had to do.

His brother told him apart from the wind and the rain it was pretty quiet outside but that he should still keep an eye on the stile that crossed the railway track.

"That's where they'll come from if they do arrive tonight. Mind you if I was them I would be tucked up in a nice cosy guest house by now."

"I wish I was," Hudson mumbled, before he clambered out of the tent.

Outside, the trees offered a little shelter but it wasn't long before he was blowing raindrops off his nose. As his eyes became accustomed to the dark he could just make out the outline of his surroundings upon which he slowly made his way from the small copse, where they were camped, and back into the middle of the ancient village site.

Out in the open it was a little lighter, and he could just about see where the railway line was in the distance, and the river beyond it. He looked for somewhere to sit down and discovered a clutch of logs nearby. Despite being pretty sodden from all the rain Hudson pulled his coat down so it covered his bottom and was about to sit down when he noticed a bright light shining out in the distance. His heart skipped a beat momentarily before realising it was a ship sailing down the river.

If that wasn't bad enough, minutes later a fox decided to scare the living daylights out of him by screeching from the nearby woods. Then something else squawked even closer.

That was the final straw. He was getting himself more and more worked up just sitting there so Hudson decided to keep his mind off things. He got up and quietly crept back to the tent. He reached inside the flap and felt for his rucksack. On the first attempt he pulled out Drake's but the next one was his. He opened it up and smiled. It had everything he needed. Placing it over his shoulder he walked back to where he had been sitting and looked for a very large hunk of wood.

At first he tried looking without the use of his torch but after a while he got fed up with the limited range the night light gave him. So he switched it on, carefully sweeping it across the floor. He soon got bored with the limitations of that and then began swirling the lengthy beam all over the place through the rain and various trees to across the field.

There were lots of pieces of wood about but not the ones Hudson was looking for. As his search continued he had quite forgotten about everything else, even where they were camped. Getting more and more frustrated by the lack of decent wood he wandered closer to Wivenhoe Woods. As he got to the edge he poured the light from his torch in through the huge dark trunks and immediately saw just what he was looking for a little way off in the distance. Grabbing his rucksack tightly by the strap he climbed over a few small bushes and wandered off inside.

A little while later back at their camp, Columbus stirred. Turning over in his sleeping bag he noticed some lights flashing outside which made him suddenly sit bolt upright. He took a deep breath to calm his nerves and slowly edged his way to the tent flap to look outside. As he did his worst fears were realised as he heard the mumbled voices of men, one of which was the unmistakable accent of a certain university professor he knew all too well.

He and his group of men were scouring the circle of trees in the pouring rain with their torches but thankfully had yet to find them.

Columbus quickly popped his head back inside and carefully prodded Drake.

"What the, is it my turn?" she said rather loudly.

He placed his hand over her mouth and then pointed outside. She knew what he meant and like Columbus had a few moments ago, started to get a nasty sick feeling in the pit of her stomach.

"We're out of sight here," he whispered. "Pack up as much as you can and we'll make a run for it through the trees."

"What about Hudson?"

"They won't hurt him. We must find the treasure first, that's the important thing."

Columbus and Drake gathered up what they needed and put them into their rucksacks. Everything else could stay with the tent.

Columbus then poked his head out of the tent flap again to discover the group had gone. Their faint chatter could just be heard above the pounding of the rain on their tent and thankfully it was now coming from the direction of the woods. Columbus breathed a sigh of relief and motioned to Drake to get moving. Both quietly slipped out of the tent but as Columbus made a quick dash for a clump of nearby trees, Drake felt a huge pair of soppy arms grab her in a bear hug.

"Got you," the man said in a rather menacing manner. Drake screamed.

On hearing her cries, Columbus turned round to see his sister trying to squirm from the huge man's grasp.

"You move any more, I'll break your bones," the man told her.

"Hey, let her go," Columbus called back.

By this time the other group of men had made their way to where all three were standing. Along with Professor Pinter there was a tall, painfully thin man with a bristly beard and a cap and two rather plump fellows, one with glasses and the other with a tattoo of a rose on the side of his face.

"There's no need for that Pole," Professor Pinter told him.

The Pole scowled back. "I told you, it's Mr Pole to you."

"Let her go Mister Pole."

The Pole reluctantly loosened his grip and Drake instinctively ran to Columbus, who gathered her up in his arms.

"I'm so sorry about my Eastern European friend but he's a bit out of control at the moment," Professor Pinter said.

"What do you want Pinter?" Columbus said angrily.

"Well that's not very nice, is it now. I thought we could pool our resources to find this burial mound."

"What burial mound?"

Professor Pinter laughed. "Come on Columbus," he said calmly. "I know why you're here. I've read Kensie's too you know and I've done a little bit of research of my own. Queen Martha of the Cathwella tribe and her magic sword."

"That's enough," The Pole interrupted. "Where is your brother?"

"We don't know," Drake replied nervously. "Honestly we don't. He was on watch and, well we thought you had captured him."

"Really Drake," Professor Pinter said. "We're not enemies you know. We can work together on this."

"Yeah right," Columbus said. "I think I've heard that one before Pinter and you tricked us then."

Professor Pinter was now starting to get angry with them. "Look I'm the professor of archaeology here, not you. Once again you Youngs are way out of your depth. You have no idea what you're dealing with."

"Nor have you."

"Enough, enough," The Pole called out. "Pinter I talk with you."

Professor Pinter told the other men to keep an eye on the children while he walked off with The Pole.

Drake and Columbus tried to hear what they were saying but could only make out a few words. Whatever they were discussing The Pole was getting very angry about it and when they finally both returned Professor Pinter looked very nervous indeed.

"Look," he began quietly to Columbus and Drake. "This guy means business. Just hand over the map and no one will get hurt."

"I thought you weren't our enemy," Columbus snarled.

"I'm not Columbus, really I'm not," Professor Pinter tried to assure him. "I know we've crossed swords in the past and I'm not exactly fans of your parents but I would never hurt you. This guy will."

"Right no more time," The Pole suddenly said and went over to Columbus and Drake.

Columbus stood in front of his sister to protect her but The Pole quickly brushed him aside, throwing him to the muddy floor.

"Please don't hurt me," Drake pleaded with him.

"Then give me the map," he said.

"There is no map," Columbus screamed from the ground, wiping the wet soil from his face.

The Pole glared at the boy. "There is a map."

Columbus turned to Professor Pinter. "Really there's no map."

"Columbus there has to be," Professor Pinter replied. "You wouldn't have made it here all by yourselves just on luck."

The Pole turned to Drake and moved forward slowly. Drake cowered as he suddenly snatched her and pulled the young girl towards him. Placing his vast arm around her neck he started to squeeze.

Drake yelled. "No, please no. Columbus, help me."

"All right, I'll get you the map."

He lifted himself from the ground and picked up Drake's rucksack. Opening it up he pulled out the plastic bag with the map inside and with his head bowed, handed it over to Professor Pinter.

"Thank you Columbus. It really is the most sensible solution. Let the experts do what they're good at, hey."

"Now let her go," Columbus growled, and The Pole obliged sending a tearful Drake running to her brother while he went over to look at the map.

Professor Pinter was already studying it intently.

"Wow. This is a find in itself. The path to the burial mound seems to start from the site of the village, which appears to be over there within that circle of trees, incredible."

The Pole grabbed the map, took it out of the plastic bag and had a look for himself.

"Be careful you oaf, that map is hundreds of years old," Professor Pinter cried out angrily. "You're getting it wet."

The Pole ignored him, preferring to look closely at the features on the map and matching them up with things that were dotted around them.

"There is the line of trees where we must go into the woods," he announced. "But not tonight. We camp here tonight."

"What about the other boy?" one of the other men asked.

"We look for him in the morning," The Pole said gruffly. "Now we sleep."

He directed Columbus and Drake back to their tent and ordered one of the men to keep a watch outside.

While Professor Pinter unfurled his own tent and began struggling to put it up in the heavy rain, The Pole simply took off his large jacket and placed it on the ground. He then lay down on the undergrowth, which was starting to get very boggy indeed, placed his head on his coat and fell fast asleep.

Inside their tent Columbus told Drake not to worry. The most important thing was to get some sleep. Hudson would be fine camped out in a den somewhere, they would come up with a plan to foil Professor Pinter and more importantly the horrible Polish man he had brought with him.

Drake, still upset from the traumatic treatment she had received, wiped her eyes and smiled.

Getting into her sleeping bag, she tried to fall asleep but her mind was too busy thinking of nasty ways to get her own back on The Pole.

Chapter Eighteen

The best thing about the next day was that it had stopped raining. The sun was out and there were even a few seagulls squawking overhead.

Columbus stepped out of his tent to find The Pole already sat next to a roaring fire holding a stick into the flames. On the end of it was a sausage coiled in a ring.

"You shouldn't really light a fire so close to the trees," Columbus told him.

"Wake up your sister, we go soon," The Pole grunted at him.

Columbus did as he was told and went back inside the tent.

A few moments later both them had got all their stuff together and were ready to go.

As they took down their tent, they could hear Pinter stirring in his nearby. He soon popped his head out and asked what time it was.

"We go in five minutes, so move it," The Pole told him finishing up the last of his sausage.

Professor Pinter shook his head forlornly and got his belongings together as quickly as he could. When he finally did come out The Pole told him there was no time to take down his tent and that he would have to leave it where it was.

"That's an expensive tent," Professor Pinter protested. "It might get stolen."

The Pole ignored him and grabbed his own rucksack. He motioned to the other three men, upon which all four of them headed off for a thin line of trees, which led into Wivenhoe Woods.

He had the map now and quite clearly the upper hand.

Columbus, Drake and Professor Pinter knew that all too well. As The Pole and his goons strode off towards the woods, they all looked at each other silently thinking the same thing. How had they got themselves into such a mess where a thug like The Pole was now controlling what should be a serious archaeological expedition? It had now become a simple dog eat dog treasure hunt in which everyone was desperately trying to be the first to get their hands on the prize.

As The Pole and his men walked off, Columbus knew he had to keep close if he was to stand any chance of outsmarting him. He told Drake to keep up with him and then jogged up to where The Pole and his men were.

Professor Pinter sighed and struggling with his rucksack also set off, squirming as he skipped through the sloshy ground, soaked from the downpours during the night. Miles would pay for this, he thought to himself. The Pole had gone too far this time, especially attacking the girl. That was definitely not on.

As he got up to Columbus and Drake he placed his hand on Drake's shoulder and smiled. Drake looked round and angrily shrugged it off.

Professor Pinter guiltily pulled his hand away. He probably deserved that, he thought.

After the narrow corridor of trees the group were soon into the woods where the ground was even muddier. The Pole stamped through it sending splatters this way and that, while Professor Pinter tried to tiptoe through the deeper bits of gloop.

As the trees got bigger and thicker all around them, they came upon a rain ditch, which was gurgling away with a swirling mass of water. As it went into a metal tunnel Columbus could hear a sudden swoosh as the water plummeted into the darkness.

"Be careful where you tread Drake," Columbus whispered to his sister. "The bank near that drain looks like it is about to fall in."

"It sounds like the water is falling down somewhere," she replied.

"Perhaps there's an underwater cave underneath us."

"Be quiet back there," The Pole called out to them.

Columbus carefully took Drake's arm and guided her past the drainage ditch.

Professor Pinter was still far too concerned with trying to avoid the big patches of mud and in doing so jumped onto the bank sending it, and him, into the fast flowing pool of water. The torrent got him straight away and almost within seconds he was sucked into the drainage pipe. Fortunately he managed to grab hold of one of the sides and screaming for help, tried to keep his head above the waters.

Drake screamed and Columbus turned to The Pole. "Help, Pinter's fallen in the drain."

The Pole turned and with a straight face told his men to get a move on.

"You can't just leave him there," Drake cried out.

But the four men just turned their backs and continued walking off.

By now Professor Pinter was really in trouble.

"Please, I can't hold on for much longer," he spluttered in desperation.

"Columbus, do something," Drake said, then remembered the rope from her rucksack.

She pulled it out quickly and handed it over to her brother. "Quick use this," she told him.

Columbus grabbed it and then made a few careful steps towards the ditch. He didn't want to fall in as well so he chose his foot holes well. By now the water seemed to be getting higher with the professor's tall frame partly blocking the metal pipe and as Columbus threw the rope he could hardly see where his head was.

The first attempt wasn't even close but after quickly pulling it back and then throwing it again, it hit him on the shoulder. Professor Pinter must have felt it slap against his side because he instinctively snatched at it, managing to hold on to it.

Columbus pulled it tight and then the professor made the very brave move of letting go of the side of the pipe to hold on to the rope with both hands.

The sudden movement jolted Columbus on the other end of the rope and he nearly lost his footing.

"Drake, come and help me, he's too heavy."

Drake did as she was told and with both them pulling hard on the rope, and Professor Pinter finally finding some shallow water to put his feet down, they managed to get him out.

Covered in mud, and soaked to the skin, Professor Pinter thanked them.

"I don't know what to say," he said gasping for air. "You saved my life."

"Don't mention it," Columbus replied. "But you owe us one now Pinter."

Sat on the muddy ground and still trying to get his breath back he smiled and nodded. "Fine. Now let's make sure that Eastern European Neanderthal doesn't get his hands on our sword."

Now Drake and Columbus smiled.

"The museum's sword, I think you mean," Drake added.

"Of course," Professor Pinter grinned. "The museum's sword."

Columbus reached out his hand and pulled Professor Pinter up.

"They went up here towards that opening," Columbus said and they all set off with a renewed vigour.

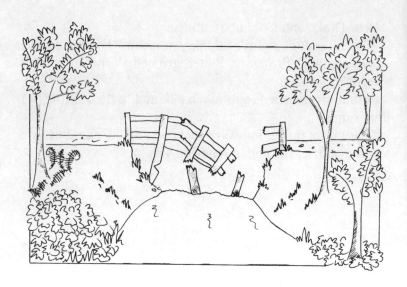

Chapter Nineteen

Their new found determination soon passed when they reached the opening. It was a small clearing that appeared to be right in the middle of the woods with a number of gorse bushes dotted around the edges and a few small grassy mounds.

It looked pretty enough but it posed the three a problem as the path had come to a crossroads. Without the map they had no idea which way to go but thankfully that didn't matter because a cry of help from up in front told them exactly which way The Pole and his men had gone.

Just outside of the clearing and back in the woods straight ahead, they could see someone hanging on to what was left of a broken bridge.

"Not again," Columbus muttered as he ran over to the bridge with the others quickly following after him.

The bridge crossed what was obviously once a small stream but due to the amount of rain that had fallen had now turned into a full-on raging torrent.

The bridge had collapsed, Columbus assumed due to the

amount of water that was gushing alongside the small banks.

The man that was holding on to one of the bridge's remaining legs was the skinny member of The Pole's gang and although Professor Pinter would have quite happily left him to his fate, Columbus knew he had to help him.

As they got to him though, he had slipped further down the bridge leg and was now hanging on for dear life.

Drake got out the rope again but before she could drop it down to him the man slipped and was sent plunging down the waters. Very quickly he was out of sight but all three heard his cries for a good few seconds later before he went silent.

"Oh my," Drake exclaimed. "You don't think."

"I'm sure he's laid up somewhere down by the river," Professor Pinter tried to reassure her. "That's where the stream will go."

"Right," he continued. "Let's think of a way of crossing this thing."

Columbus was way ahead of him.

"Give me the rope," he told Drake, and then he began shinning up a nearby tree. Half way up he tied the rope to a rather large branch, checked that it was secure and then clambered back down.

The rope had unfurled down in front of them and Drake knew exactly what Columbus intended.

"Come on, we'll swing over," he told them both.

"Well I haven't done this since I was a kid, I might be a bit rusty," Professor Pinter said nervously.

"Well don't be too rusty Pinter or you'll end up like that other bloke."

"Indeed," Professor Pinter replied looking down at the fast flowing water underneath him.

"Well here goes," he said before taking a long run at the rope.

He stretched out his hands, grabbed hold of the rope and lifted his legs as he swung out over the water but instead of leaping off on the other side he swung back to where Columbus and Drake were standing.

"You're supposed to let go," Drake told him.

"I know, I know, I'm just getting used to the sensation," he replied agitated by the whole experience.

"Look I'll show you how it's done," Drake said bravely as she leapt at the rope with some grace and crossed the collapsed bridge with ease.

Columbus was next and once over told the professor to throw the bags to them.

"Now you," Columbus shouted over the noise of the gushing water.

Professor Pinter crossed himself, despite not being remotely religious, and then ran towards the rope. He got hold of it and the momentum of his run sent him flying over. As he got to the other side Columbus grabbed hold of him as Drake shouted to let go. He did and fell to the ground with a thud.

"Ouch, that hurt," he said.

"That was pathetic Pinter," Columbus said giggling.

"Well at least I'm over," he replied and he got up and dusted himself down. "Right on we go," and they all set off again.

Several paths led off the main route but Columbus told them he was sure the way forward was the route to take. He turned out to be right as within a few hundred yards they came upon the rest of The Pole's men laying flat on their backs and out cold.

Next to them was a rather large log, which by the looks of things had fallen from above and knocked the two men out.

Drake knelt down next to them and noticed one of them had a rather large gash in the side of his head.

"They're breathing, but this guy's bleeding," she told the others. "We should get help."

Suddenly from behind a tree The Pole appeared and grabbed Drake from behind.

"Oh no you don't," Professor Pinter cried as he lunged

towards him only for The Pole to thrust out a fist which connected with the professor's chin with an almighty crunch.

Professor Pinter slumped to the floor in a heap.

Columbus looked at the burly man and asked him what he wanted them to do now.

"You've got the map, why do you need us?"

"There appears to be a lot of accidents. I do not want something unpleasant to happen to me also."

"What the Dickens do you expect us to do about it?" Columbus said.

"Where is your brother?"

"We told you, we don't know," Drake said, trying to wriggle free from The Pole's iron like grip.

Just as he pulled her closer a large plank of wood swung down from the treetops. The Pole ducked and threw Drake into its path but fortunately she managed to dodge it as well.

As The Pole got to his feet he spotted Hudson clinging to the tree from where the plank had come from.

"There you are my little friend," he called out to him. "The game is up for you now, come down here."

"No fear, you big brute," Hudson replied. "I've placed traps all over the place and one of them is going to get you sooner or later."

"Then I kill your brother and sister," The Pole said, producing a gun from his jacket pocket and pointing it at Columbus and Drake.

"Actually I was only kidding about the traps, there are no more," Hudson said hurriedly.

"Well you come down and prove it," The Pole told him.

Hudson clambered down and joined his brother and sister who both patted him on the back.

"Good work Hud," Drake smiled at him.

"You look tired bro," Columbus added.

"Well I've been a bit busy," Hudson replied.

"So I see," Columbus said. "Was the bridge you as well?"

Hudson nodded. "Yes that was my piece de resistance, I

just got..."

"Quiet," The Pole interrupted them. "You have caused unnecessary delay already, no more fun, let's go."

He ordered Hudson to take the lead just so he could be sure there were no more traps and as they were about to set off Professor Pinter came around.

"Hudson, where did you come from?" he asked wearily shaking his head.

Hudson pointed upwards.

"Oh," Professor Pinter frowned.

"Come on Professor," The Pole said. "You can lead the way with the boy. I might need you when we get to the burial mound."

Professor Pinter got to his feet and joined the group.

"What's with Pinter?" Hudson whispered to Columbus.

"He's one of us," he replied.

"What!"

"It's a long story, I'll tell you later."

So the group set off for the fourth time with Hudson and the professor leading the way, followed by Columbus and Drake and then finally The Pole calling out the directions from behind, map in one hand and gun in the other.

"Past a tree with two trunks," The Pole called out as they came to another crossroads and sure enough within metres they were upon it.

"Now take the path that goes right," he said.

It wasn't long before he was barking out more orders, this time to stop.

This they did as he studied the map closer.

Then for the first time that morning, the Youngs and Professor Pinter caught a glimpse of a rather wonderful sight. The Pole looked perplexed. He looked at the map a second time, then a third but couldn't make out what the directions meant as the route looked like it spiralled round and round. But there were no paths that spiralled round.

There was a path that forked into two and one off to the

right but they all went dead straight.

The Pole shook his head again and then reluctantly called the professor over.

"What's wrong Mr Pole, are you lost," Professor Pinter said smiling.

"Shut up or I put a hole through you," The Pole replied angrily, pointing the pistol into his face.

"Hey point that thing somewhere else, I'll help you," Professor Pinter replied.

Pinter looked at the map and also looked confused. "I don't know where it goes," he said. "We're on a hill here, look there's the river below. Perhaps it means we should go down the hill."

Columbus walked over with Hudson and also entered the discussion.

"When I was studying it I thought it might mean the path goes underground. Perhaps there's an entrance in the side of the hill."

While all this was going on Drake suddenly felt the need to answer a call of nature and told the group she was going for a pee.

The rest of them were so busy looking at the map and suggesting alternative routes that no one took any notice of her.

She shrugged her shoulders and looked around for a tree that had a big enough trunk to give her some privacy, and then headed off for it.

Crouching down she rested her hand against the bark, only for the trunk to give way, sending her toppling down inside it.

Chapter Twenty

When Drake finally opened her eyes she saw absolutely nothing. It was pitch black. She knew she had fallen but had no idea how far or where she had landed up. She brushed her hair from her eyes and wiped the pieces of dirt that she could feel stuck to the side of her face. Then she slowly got to her feet only to bang her head on the low roof.

Great, now her head was throbbing, and she still couldn't see a damn thing. She knelt down and felt around her, finally discovering what appeared to be a step. A few inches beyond the step was another step and gently Drake made her way down what eventually turned out to be a whole flight.

At the bottom the light improved a little and Drake could see that the bottom of the steps led to the entrance to a long tunnel. The source of the light was coming from what looked like the end of the tunnel so she began to carefully walk along it as quietly as she could.

As she got closer to the light she could make out strange drawings on the walls. Some were strange symbols, others were lines of text that looked a lot like the ancient Cathwella language she first saw on the map.

The most marvellous picture of them all was one of a woman battling with a huge dragon. With bright long flowing red hair, a glorious red tunic and wielding a huge sword that looked as though it was glowing with fire, Drake immediately knew it was Queen Martha.

A wave of excitement flowed through her. Had she found the way to Queen Martha's tomb? And more important than that, may be her magical sword?

A few further yards down the tunnel and her question was answered.

The tunnel finally opened up into a massive cavern surrounded by rocky outcrops and large boulders that looked like they were stuck to the walls with glue.

At the far end of the cave Drake saw where the light was coming from, and it was from a most unusual place, a small underground lake. The water was a brilliant silvery white, twinkling like a million stars. In fact the effect was so bright Drake ended up squinting at the wonderful, mystical sight. Then she saw what was in the middle of the lake, a grassy mound with a large rock on the top and then she saw what was in the rock.

She took a deep breath and felt a tingle tip-toe up her spine.

It was Queen Martha's sword, its blade impaled in the rock just like the way King Arthur's sword was in all those films.

She sniggered at the coincidence and then suddenly wondered what to do next.

There was Queen Martha's sword glistening from the light from the lake almost daring Drake to come over and pluck it out from its resting place.

But something wasn't right. The silence in the cave was eerie and the way the water hadn't so much as rippled, and yet still twinkled, started to unsettle her. At first she thought it might be a sheet of ice but the cave was positively boiling hot.

Eventually curiosity got the better of her and she picked up a pebble from the ground and threw it into the water. That really freaked her out because as soon as the pebble hit the water a huge wave rose up and a massive serpent like tale splashed too and fro before sinking beneath the waves.

Right, not a good idea, thought Drake, and made a mental note not to throw anything else into the water.

Chapter Twenty-One

Above ground Columbus, Hudson, Professor Pinter and The Pole were searching the surrounding area for her.

It was while looking for the path to the burial mound they heard her scream, sending them scurrying back to where she had been standing.

"She said she was going for a pee," Columbus informed the others.

"Well, where would a young girl go to pee?" Professor Pinter asked out loud.

"Duh, a tree or a bush," Hudson replied.

"Great, that narrows it down," Columbus added.

"Shut up you fools," The Pole interrupted. "It came from up there," he said, pointing to a couple of large beech trees.

But when they got to the trees there was no sign of her.

After a few minutes of looking around Columbus, frustrated through worry, slammed his hand against one of the tree trunks sending a large portion of the bark swinging inside of itself, and then quickly slamming back shut.

'A secret door,' he whispered to himself.

He looked at the others to see if they had witnessed what he had just seen and breathed a sigh of relief when he realised they had not.

He then waited a few minutes before suggesting they move onto another area to search.

"I think it came from over there actually," and he headed off from the tree grabbing Hudson with him.

When they were enough of a distance away from the professor and The Pole he whispered what had happened a few moments earlier.

"Wow, you're kidding," Hudson said loudly.

"Shoosh you idiot, keep it down," Columbus told him. "We have to wait while they're busy looking over here and then we'll quietly go back and slip inside the tree."

"Cool," Hudson replied excitedly.

Soon the other two had joined them and were busy scouring behind various trees and bushes. When they were out of sight behind a particularly big holly bush Columbus motioned to Hudson to go back to the secret door.

They crept back as quietly as they could over the leaves and twigs that littered the ground of the woods.

Once at the tree Columbus took a look around the trunk to see where the others were and safe in the knowledge the coast was clear placed his hand on the tree and pushed the secret door open.

Hudson giggled with excitement.

"Shut up you loon," Columbus hushed at him.

"Sorry," Hudson whispered back and they both stepped inside the tree.

As soon as the door closed behind them they were plunged into darkness.

"Torch Hudson."

"Torch?"

"The one I gave you last night when you went on watch."

"Oh yeah it's in my bag."

"Well can you get it out?"

"I don't have my bag with me."

"Well where is it?"

"I left it out there," Hudson replied sheepishly.

"Great," Columbus sighed. "Well we can't go back out there now, we'll just have to feel our..ahhhh," he yelled, as he slipped down the steps.

Hudson heard a thud and then asked his brother whether he was alright.

"Ow, that hurt," Columbus moaned. "Watch out there's some steps."

"I kind of guessed that," Hudson replied from the top before feeling his way down the first step.

Just as he got down to see where it was, a brilliant shaft of light suddenly appeared from behind him illuminating the way.

He could see the old stone steps and right at the bottom of them his brother sitting down rubbing his head.

"That's better," he declared. "I can see where I'm going now."

Then he realised where the light was coming from. Somebody had opened the secret door in the tree trunk and a familiar posh voice told him who it was.

"There you both are," the professor called down. "I was wondering where you had got to."

"Don't suppose you're on your own," Columbus shouted up at him.

"Fraid not," he replied as The Pole pushed him to one side.

"Nice try boys," he smiled. "Right Pinter down you go. I feel we are getting closer. The sword will soon be mine."

Pinter clambered through the door along with The Pole and then walked down the steps to join the others.

As The Pole stepped inside the tiny tunnel the door slammed shut behind him and they were in the dark again.

"I can't see a damned thing," he shouted out.

"Quick grab him," Columbus called out from down below.

"And how do you propose I do that without the torch in my bag," Hudson replied. "I can't see a thing either. Oh is that you Pinter," he added, after bumping into someone's arm.

"No it isn't," The Pole replied and then shined a beam of light into his face. "I'm glad I picked up your bags. I thought they might be useful."

He then pointed Hudson's torch downwards to see his way down the stairs and spotted Columbus at the bottom.

"Ah there you are. Right this way I believe," he pointed towards the entrance of the cave.

The group moved slowly down the long tunnel and they too noticed the cave paintings on the walls.

"These are incredible Columbus, don't you think," Professor Pinter uttered in pure amazement.

Columbus couldn't believe his eyes either. "Look there's a picture of the village."

"There's one of the map over here," Hudson pointed out.

"Wow, look at that," Columbus replied. "And look at this one."

Further along there was a stone mound with a sword encased in it. On top there looked like a man trying to pull it out and another group of men running away from it.

"What do you think that means?" Columbus said pointing to it.

"Stay away from the sword?" Hudson offered up an answer. "They certainly don't look too keen to stick around it."

The Pole was more concerned with the light at the end of the tunnel than the drawings on the wall, especially as it got brighter and brighter as the four of them walked on.

"Quiet," he scolded them. "We do not know what is up there."

Bearing in mind the cave drawing they had just seen they took heed of his warning. There could be anything up ahead of them. Whatever it was, both Columbus and Hudson hoped their sister was safe from it.

As they reached the end of the long tunnel their walking pace had reduced to almost a tip toe, nervously trying to make as little noise as possible.

When they entered into the huge cave the spectacle that greeted them threw all those nerves to one side.

"The sword," Columbus muttered.

"Pon my word, that is a sight beyond anyone's wildest dreams," Professor Pinter added.

"Hang on a minute," Hudson said as he reached inside his rucksack. "This is worth a picture."

He got out his brown boxed camera and pointed it at the lake, mound and particularly the sword that sat on top of the lot. He snapped one and then asked the others whether they wanted to pose in front of it for the next shot.

"We have no time for this stupidity," The Pole said angrily. "We must get the sword."

"I'll get it," Columbus volunteered.

The Pole checked the surrounding area. He didn't trust the boy one little bit but then he had his gun and apart from another tunnel to their left and the one they had just come down there appeared to be no other way out.

He also didn't fancy crossing the lake. He liked to see his enemies up close and personal, whatever they were, and with the light shining up through the water anything could be lurking in there. No, on second thoughts the boy could go.

Columbus was surprised by his decision and with a great deal of excitement headed off to the waters' edge.

It was very strange how the water just appeared to be standing so still and yet was still twinkling extraordinarily brightly but he shrugged it off and went to step into the water.

Chapter Twenty-Two

"Stop," a voice yelled from the opening of the other tunnel.

It was Drake. She had been watching them very closely up until now, looking for a chance to perhaps get The Pole off guard and knock him out.

However seeing her brother about to make his way into the lake where she had just seen some kind of monster splashing about, she knew she had no choice but to warn him off.

"I wouldn't go in there if I was you bro," she told him. "There's something in the water."

"What kind of something?" Columbus asked her nervously, stepping quickly away from the waters' edge.

"A dragon," Drake replied dramatically. "Like the one in the drawings."

"Ha," The Pole snorted. "No such things as Dragons. Go on boy," he waved Columbus on.

Columbus stood firm.

"I said get on with it. Get in the water."

"Actually I don't think I will Mr Pole. Why don't you have

a go?"

The Pole pulled out his gun and shot Columbus straight through the leg sending him crashing to the floor writhing in pain.

"You monster," Professor Pinter yelled.

"Columbus," Hudson and Drake called out as they rushed to him.

Blood was starting to seep out of the side of his leg but thankfully The Pole had not hit anything too life threatening.

"It is merely a flesh wound," he said. "But the next one will be much more severe. You," he pointed to Hudson. "It is time for you to go across."

"Not ruddy likely," Hudson replied.

The Pole raised his pistol and aimed it at Columbus again.

"Then I have no choice but to.."

"All right, all right I'm going."

Hudson knew it was no use. He turned forlornly to Drake and smiled.

"I'll be all right. I'm a pretty good swimmer, I'll get across in no time."

He walked towards the lake breathing very heavily and thought about the best way to approach the problem.

He could wade across very slowly so as not to disturb the monster, or perhaps even float on his back, kicking every now again to propel himself to the other side.

No, the monster would either, see him, smell him or hear him. Best thing for it, Hudson reckoned, was to take a huge run up, dive in and then swim as fast as he could.

And that's exactly what he did. Taking a huge breath he sprinted to the edge and threw himself in. As he rose to the surface he frantically kicked his legs and pulled his arms in and out of the water.

Drake and Columbus watched in amazement as their brave little brother furiously made his way across the lake.

He was just a few metres away from the mound, when they saw the water suddenly rise at one end.

A look of horror came over them all as the surge lifted up and quickly started to make its way towards where Hudson was swimming.

Drake called out to him but his splashes prevented him from hearing her.

As the water got closer Drake turned her head away in fright and Columbus felt as though his heart was about to explode from his chest.

Everyone stopped breathing for a second, except Hudson who was unaware of what was going on behind him.

If he had of done, he would surely have frozen with sheer fright but thankfully he did not.

The water got closer and bigger and as Hudson was placing his hands on the mound to lift himself out, it hit him.

He felt the huge tide lift him up and in a rather impressive somersault, any gymnast would have been proud of, he landed quite neatly on his backside on the mound.

Columbus let out a huge sigh of relief and told his sister it was all right to look.

As the waters died down as quickly as they had risen up, Hudson brushed himself down and smiled over at his brother and sister who were still white with fear.

"Told you I would make it," he joked.

"Well done. That was great swimming," Drake called back.

"Now get the sword," The Pole shouted.

"All right, all right," Hudson replied as he got to his feet and walked over to the rock.

"How is he going to get back?" Drake whispered to Columbus.

"With any luck that sword will have the magic powers it says it has in the book. If it doesn't, I honestly don't know. Ah this leg," he said still wincing with pain.

"Does it hurt a lot?"

"I have just been shot in the leg Drake, of course it hurts a lot."

116

"Sorry," she replied.

Over on the grassy mound Hudson was struggling with the sword. He pulled at it several times but nothing was happening.

"It's stuck. It won't budge an inch," he cried out.

The Pole pointed his gun at the professor and told him to go over and help Hudson with the sword.

"You must be joking. I'm not going anywhere near that lake."

"Then I shoot the boy," The Pole declared menacingly.

"Go on then, see if I care," Professor Pinter replied.

"Pinter!" Drake cried out.

"Don't worry, he's not going to shoot him."

"Then I shoot you," The Pole said defiantly.

"Well that's not going to get you very far is it," Professor Pinter told him calmly. "If you shoot me I can't very well go and help Hudson with the sword, can I."

The Pole thought for a while.

Pinter obviously wasn't going to budge and it was no use sending the other two over. Columbus couldn't walk and the girl would be useless at lifting the sword out of the stone. There was nothing for it but to cross the lake himself. He loaded his gun with more bullets and picked some stones up from the ground. He would throw them into the water before he went in and then shoot whatever it was that was below.

As he got to the edge of the lake he chucked some small stones to the far side of the lake and then waited.

Nothing.

He threw a few more and still not so much as a ripple.

He decided to get some bigger ones and then chucked those into the lake. This time the water moved and convinced he saw something swish about just underneath the surface, he aimed and fired a whole round of shots into the waves. The swirling water bubbled and then the lake turned red.

"Ha, I have him," he called out.

Not wanting to waste this opportunity he leapt into the water and began wading over to the mound.

Half way across, the water was too deep to put his feet down so he began to swim across, lightly kicking and pulling his arms through the water very gently in a breast-stroke-like fashion.

Apart from his own tiny splashes from where he was kicking, the lake was perfectly still, but as soon as he had completed just a few strokes it suddenly rose up again, all around him like a watery cage. Then just as quickly the waves engulfed him like a giant fist grabbing a ball and pulled him under with an almighty whoosh.

In seconds the water was calm.

Chapter Twenty-Three

Drake and Columbus looked at each other in astonishment and then back to the place where The Pole had been swimming moments earlier.

Just as they did a small black, hairy bundle popped up from the waters below and began bobbing about the surface.

"Well I never," Professor Pinter exclaimed. "I never knew he wore a wig."

He then turned to Columbus. "Well what the bejeezers do we do now?"

"You're the adult, you think of something."

"Well can someone do something," Hudson called out from the island. "I'm getting a bit scared over here."

"Oh for crying out loud," Drake suddenly said. "You want something done, let a girl do it."

"Drake don't be silly," Columbus told her but it was too late. Drake had already set off and was soon walking through the shallowly waters of the lake with her eyes kept firmly shut.

Everyone watched in stunned silence as she made her way further into the water. She soon lost her footing and, like The Pole had done so earlier, began swimming over to the grassy mound. As she got closer to the tiny island Hudson went over to the edge to help her out and keep a close eye on any movement.

"It's all quiet Drake, keep going," he willed her on.

Eventually she made it and Hudson grabbed her arms and pulled her out.

"Well done," he said very relieved and gave her a big hug.

"Crikey Hud if that's what it takes to get a hug off you I might cross monster infested waters more often. Right let's have a go at this sword."

"It's pretty tough work," Hudson said but as soon as Drake had placed her hands on the sword's handles the thing slipped smoothly out from the rock.

"How the hell did you do that?" Hudson said stunned by what he had just seen.

Drake was equally amazed. "It just came away from the sides."

She lifted the sword up to show Columbus and the professor what she had done.

"Brilliant," Columbus called out. "Now get back over here."

Suddenly there was a flash of light and Drake disappeared, only for her to appear on the other side of the lake right next to Columbus.

"What the.." Columbus said. "How did you do that?"

"I don't know," Drake replied. "I just thought about being over here with you and then it happened."

"Well can you think about getting me over there with you too," Hudson shouted from the island.

Drake held up the sword and in another flash of light Hudson had vanished from the island and reappeared, just like she had done, right next to them.

"Woah, that was weird," he said feeling slightly disorientated from the experience.

"You couldn't point that thing at my leg could you," Columbus asked his sister.

"I'll give it a go," she replied and directed the blade at her brother's leg and thought about it being healed.

A third flash of light filled the cave around them and all of them looked down at the gash where The Pole had shot him. There was nothing there.

"It's gone, I feel fine," Columbus cried out.

"It is a magic sword," Professor Pinter said. "Be careful Drake, that thing has powers none of us can possibly understand. I think you should give to me."

As he went to grab it from her the lake burst into life again with another huge wave rising up into a massive wall of water which swirled around and around before sinking back down into a whirlpool. From inside the swirling water a knarled head with scaly pointy ears emerged gradually at first, and then very quickly.

Within a matter of seconds a huge brown and green speckled dragon was scarily starring at them with its bright yellow eyes.

"Crikey O'Reilly," Hudson said stunned with what was standing in front of them.

"I told you there was a dragon," Drake added.

"And boy, do we believe you now," Columbus replied.

"What do you think it wants?" Hudson whispered.

"I've never met a dragon before," Drake replied. "Perhaps he just wants a chat."

The dragon moved his head from side to side as though he was examining each of them in great detail. When it got to

Drake, it paused and then moved closer to get a better look.

Trembling, Drake muttered for the dragon to leave her alone but then it did something very odd indeed. It spoke.

"It is you," it boomed. "I have been waiting a long time for your return."

"Crikey O'Reilly a talking dragon," Hudson exclaimed.

"Yes because a dragon on its own isn't unusual at all," Drake replied. "Why shouldn't a dragon talk," she continued. "My question is what does it want with me?"

The dragon moved slowly out of the water and the Youngs and the professor moved several steps back.

"I am ready for you this time your majesty but this time I will be the victor," the dragon bellowed at Drake.

"Well, what do you think that means?" Columbus whispered to the others.

"It thinks Drake is Queen Martha," Hudson whispered back.

"It's got pretty bad eyesight if it does," Columbus replied. "Anyway I thought Queen Martha killed the dragon."

"That was only a myth," Drake interrupted them. "She obviously didn't finish off the job and now it wants revenge. Anyway shoosh, it's moving again."

The dragon lifted its long tail and swept it towards Drake.

She instinctively lifted the sword, still firmly gripped inside her right hand, and waved it to fend off the dragon's advances.

A bolt of light streamed from the tip of the sword and glanced a blow on the dragon's side.

The effect was immediate as the beast let out a piercing cry and then shook its head in pain.

Hudson turned to his sister, "I think you made it mad."

"I didn't mean to," Drake said nervously.

The dragon was more wary of Drake now and sidled slowly around to one of the tunnels that led from the cave, all the time keeping a firm eye on Drake and the sword.

At the entrance he swiped his claws at the rocks above it

sending them crashing down and closing it up completely.

"He's trying to trap us in," Pinter said to the others. "Quick make for the other tunnel."

But before they could even start the dragon had lifted up a huge boulder and blasted it against the wall opposite them closing that one up as well.

"Use the sword," Columbus told Drake.

She pointed it at the rock fall to clear the obstruction but the dragon was behind them and with a swift swipe of its claws again had grabbed Drake, lifting her high into the air.

She screamed and desperately hacked the sword into the dragon's flesh but one squeeze from the monster was all it took for the breath to be taken clean out of her.

As Drake slumped over the hand of the dragon, her grip on the sword was loosened, sending it falling to the cave floor.

Hudson was quick to run over and grab it, and as soon as he had it in his hands, pointed it at the dragon's head.

"Die beast," he shouted angrily but nothing happened.

The dragon laughed. "You do not have the power to use Queen Martha's sword. Only the queen of the Cathwellas can destroy me and I am about to destroy her."

"But she's not the queen of the Cathwellas," Columbus shouted up at the dragon. "She's just a girl from Wellsbridge. Queen Martha died centuries ago."

The dragon starred menacingly down at Columbus and the others. "Yes but her ancestors live on. Now give me the sword and I will be free at last."

"Free from what?" Columbus asked. "You killed those boys so you're not trapped here."

The dragon grimaced. "Don't remind me. They tasted horrible but I was desperate for food. I hadn't eaten in months.

"Yes I'm free to roam wherever I please," the dragon snarled. "But I will never be free from death until the people that can defeat me are destroyed."

"Let Drake go," Columbus pleaded. "We'll give you the sword and then you can just get rid of it. No one will be able to kill you then."

The dragon was getting frustrated. "You think I trust you pitiful humans. I have been waiting for someone like her to release it, and now she has I can track down the rest of the Cathwellas and free myself from their threat once and for all. Now give me the sword."

"What do you think?" Columbus quietly muttered to the others.

Hudson looked astonished at his brother. "You're not suggesting we give it to him."

Columbus scowled at Hudson. "No you dunderhead. What shall we do?"

"Don't you think something is a little strange here," Pinter interrupted.

"What apart from the talking dragon and our sister being the queen of the Cathwellas," Columbus replied.

Pinter smiled. "No seriously Columbus don't you think it is odd it hasn't just taken the sword. This thing could kill us all quite easily if it wanted to and yet it is asking us for the sword. Why do you think that is?"

There was a brief pause before Hudson asked him. "Well why hasn't it killed us all then?"

"Oh I don't know," Pinter replied. "It is a little odd though."

"Great," Columbus sighed. "That really helps us out."

"Actually Col." Hudson suddenly had a thought. "That does help us out. Perhaps all the descendants of the Cathwellas have special powers too."

"What!" Columbus said.

"Well if Drake is the queen we must be related to them as well."

"Why can't we use the sword then clever clogs?"

"Wait a minute," Pinter interrupted them again. "It can't kill you. Remember how Hudson escaped it swimming across the lake and Drake as well, now look at it."

All three looked up at the dragon as it stood motionless

staring at them.

"It's just waiting there," Pinter continued. "Because the only way it can get the sword is by killing you and for some reason it cannot do that."

At that very moment Drake, still slumped inside the dragon's fist, started to move, slowly regaining consciousness. Wearily she looked up to see the dragon right in front of her and immediately screamed.

With its eyes fixed on the others this surprised the dragon a little and with a little jolt he instinctively unfurled his claws and Drake dropped to the ground with a heavy thump.

The dragon went to grab her again but Columbus sprinted towards her to put himself in the way.

"Move or I'll squash you like a fly," the dragon bellowed at him.

"I don't think so," Columbus said defiantly and then turning to Drake told her to make a run for it.

The dragon grabbed Columbus to move him out of the way and then went to reach for Drake with his other hand but it was too late. She speedily rejoined Hudson and Pinter, and grabbed the sword right away, pointing it at the dragon.

"Let my brother go," she shouted up at the monster.

"Give me the sword or he dies," the dragon replied holding her brother just underneath the roof of the cave. "I can crush him to death very easily."

"Don't listen to him Drake," Columbus called down. "He can't kill us."

"What, are you sure?" Drake answered back.

Hudson nodded. "We think so. You're the queen of the Cathwellas and we're Cathwellas too, and because of that he can't do us in. Oh except with the sword, so whatever you do, don't let him have the sword."

Columbus started grimacing with pain as the dragon's grip got tighter. "Can you hurry up please it's starting to hurt a bit. I know he can't kill us but he can certainly make it painful."

"Believe me I'll do it," the dragon threatened.

"Don't you think it would have done us all in by now if it could have done," Pinter said calmly to Drake.

Things were all very confusing for Drake. She had just recovered from being nearly crushed to death by a dragon and now her older brother was in the same predicament.

If that wasn't enough she was being told she was the queen of the Cathwella tribe, her brothers were members of the tribe and the dragon had to be killed.

She had never thought of herself as much of a fighter but as her brother's screams grew louder she was starting to think it was about time she did.

"For pity's sake Drake just blast it," Hudson told her.

And that's exactly what she did, lifting the sword high above her head and aiming it right between the dragon's eyes.

A bolt of lightening blasted out from the sword and sped towards the beast. The creature yelped a desperate cry and as the light collided with it, Columbus was thrown to the ground and everyone was blinded by the biggest flash of light yet.

Then there was silence.

When they finally opened their eyes, the dragon was gone, without so much of a trace of it left anywhere in the cave.

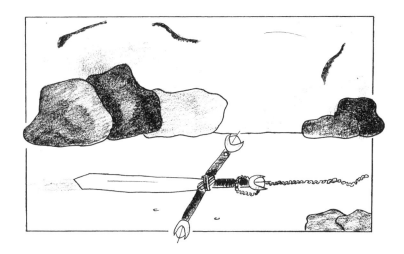

Chapter Twenty-Four

Drake looked around at her brothers with a rather guilty look. She had never killed anything in her life before, not even a fly, and now she had despatched a dragon.

"Now what do we do?" she asked them.

"Well for a start you could get us all out of here," Professor Pinter told her.

Drake looked around to the spot where the dragon had slung the huge boulder in front of the tunnel and then pointed the sword at it.

Nothing happened.

She thrust it towards the rock with more vigour this time, but again nothing.

"It doesn't work," Drake declared nervously.

"Perhaps it's done its job already," Professor Pinter announced mysteriously.

"What do you mean?" Columbus asked him.

"Maybe the sword was created to kill the dragon and when it did that it ceased to have a purpose, its magic powers passing with it."

"Well who knows what's going on," Columbus sighed.

"What I do know is we're stuck in this cave with no way of getting out."

There was a long pause while everyone thought about their predicament until Drake spoke up.

"What about the lake. It must lead out to the river. We could dive down and see if there is a way out underwater."

"Good idea," Columbus replied and then volunteered to jump in.

He stepped up to the edge and quickly dived in.

A few moments later he resurfaced shaking his head.

"No chance," he announced pulling himself out of the water. "I found the tunnel but it looks like it goes for miles."

"Oooh oooh," Hudson jumped about suddenly. "I know how we are supposed to get out. Remember that picture we saw on the wall of the stick man holding the sword and the other stick men running away?"

"Yes," Columbus replied a little unsure of where Hudson was going with this.

"Well may be they weren't running away from the sword because it was scary. May be the guy was sticking the sword back in the stone so the others could escape."

Columbus shook his head. "Where do you get these ideas from? Oh well it can't hurt I suppose. Who wants to go over and put the sword back in the rock?"

"I'll go," Drake volunteered as she lifted the sword above her head and waded into the water. Soon she was over the other side and by the slit in the rock where she had pulled out the sword moments earlier.

"Here goes," she called out and she carefully positioned the blade's tip into the crack and slowly let it fall back into place.

As it did Drake was sure she heard a small click. She called out again to say that it was in and then the group waited.

They didn't have to wait very long for after a few seconds from the sword going in, a deafening cracking sound came from what was a bare wall behind the boys on the other side of the lake.

They spun around to see two large slabs of rock split apart from each other to reveal another tunnel.

"I told you," Hudson squealed with excitement.

"Come on let's get out of here," Columbus said as he made his way towards the entrance. Then he remembered something. "Don't forget the sword, Drake. It may not have special powers anymore but it's still the archaeological find of the year, that's for sure."

Drake went to lift it back out of the rock but as soon as she did the slabs of rock that had opened up when she had put it in, started to close again.

"Woah, Woah there Drake," Columbus called out. "Put it back in, put it back in."

Drake quickly did as she was told and the slabs moved back in the opposite direction again.

"Blast," Columbus exclaimed. "It looks like we'll have to go without our prize again. Leave it there Drake and come on back over."

Drake was as disappointed as Columbus and as she made her way back to the lake's edge she looked over her shoulder and thought how wonderful it would have been to go back home with the sword of Queen Martha.

After all it was now a family heirloom.

As she swam back over the others made their way to the tunnel but as they did the entrance appeared to close up again.

Columbus looked back over to the rock but the sword was still in place.

"It must be on some kind of timer," Hudson said and then looked at his sister struggling to get out of the water. "Hurry up Drake the cave's closing up."

Columbus instinctively looked for something to block the two slabs of rock while Drake scrambled to her feet and sprinted towards them.

"Here help me with this boulder," Columbus called over to Pinter and the both of them lifted a huge stone in between the doors which were now coming together quite quickly.

They then jumped through the now narrow space themselves and waited for the stone to leave enough space for Drake to squeeze through.

But it didn't. As soon as the doors met it they crushed it with such force a blast of stone ash blew into Drake's face as the wall closed right up in front of her.

The last thing she heard was a scream of "No" from her brothers on the other side and then there was silence.

Columbus tried looking at his brother but it was pitch black again.

"Are you there Hud?" he called out.

"Yeah Col, I'm here," Hudson replied starting to cry. "Drake," he started.

"I know Hud, I know."

"I hate to break up this rather touching show of affection for one's sister," Professor Pinter called out in the darkness. "But if we're going to help Drake we have to get out of here ourselves. Now who has got the torch? I can't see a thing."

Before Columbus could angrily answer, a very familiar noise, which made them all hold their hands to their ears, took hold of them and a shaft of light appeared from where the slabs of rock had just closed.

As it opened up completely once more Columbus looked into the cave to see a smiling Drake standing over the sword.

"I thought if it worked the first two times it was going to work a third," she shouted. "We just need to find a way of getting it back in the rock in order to give me enough time to get through the tunnel."

"Some kind of contraption then," Hudson smiled back at her. "Don't you worry, I have just the thing."

While the entrance closed up again Hudson reached into his and Columbus' rucksacks and pulled out two long reels of rope.

"Right we need to hang this quite high so we can drop the sword back into the stone," Hudson mumbled as he looked up at the walls of the cave, quickly spotting a small outcrop of rocks that looked perfect for his plan.

He uncurled the pieces of rope and then tied them together.

Giving one end to Columbus he then climbed up the face of the cave where he passed the rope around a rock.

Climbing back down he then crossed the lake with the rope in his hand until he got to the grass mound where Drake was sitting waiting for him.

"All right sis now all I need is some kind of frame to hang this rope over the rock," Hudson muttered. "Oooh, Oooh, my bits of wood."

Hudson handed over the other end of the rope to Drake and then dived back into the water. On the other side he asked both Columbus and Pinter for their bootlaces and then reached into his backpack.

Pulling out a number of pieces of wood he had picked up during his activities the night before, he then excitedly jogged back to the lake's edge and crossed it once again.

On the grassy mound he assembled his frame using the wood and all the bootlaces, including his and Drake's, and then carefully positioned it over the rock. He then got Drake to hand him over the rope she had been hanging on to all this time, looped it through the frame and tied it to the sword's handle.

"Now careful Drake," he said. "Take the sword and just put the tip of it into the slot.

"Right hold it there," he said suddenly as she did as she was told.

He then called over to Columbus to take up the slack on the rope so it was tight and the sword was left hanging in place.

"Brilliant," he called out and then carefully Hudson pushed the frame gently into the mound so it stood firm, leaving just enough space to allow the sword to dangle in the air when Drake took her hands away from it.

"Right Drake you can let go now," he told her.

Holding her breath she did so and thankfully the sword remained where it was.

He then told Columbus to gently let the rope slip through his hands to check if the weight of the sword would drop it in to place. As he did Hudson watched nervously as Queen Martha's glistening sword did what he hoped it would.

"Super," he called out again. "Let's get back to the other side."

As they did Columbus was starting to feel the strain of holding the sword and called out to his brother and sister to get a move on.

Meanwhile Professor Pinter congratulated Hudson on their endeavours as he went back to the entrance to wait for it to open again.

When Hudson got back to where Columbus was, he dipped into his rucksack and pulled out his camera again.

"Now I've got to have a picture of this," he declared as he pointed it at the contraption.

"Do you mind Hudson," Columbus said, the strain starting to show on his face.

"Sorry," Hudson replied, quickly placing the camera's stringed strap over his head so it hung around his neck.

Now they were all ready, but just as Columbus was about to let the rope go, he had an idea.

"Wait a minute. What's stopping us from pulling the sword back after it has dropped into the rock."

"But the entrance will close," Drake replied.

"We'll be through it already, holding on to the rope," Columbus smiled.

"Yes but we'll all need to pull it," Hudson added. "It's pretty heavy and it's got a long way to travel."

"Well you've got nothing to lose," Professor Pinter said with a glint in his eye.

"Right grab a piece of the rope then," Columbus told the others and when they each had a hold of it he gave the order to let it slip through their fingers.

In the distance the sword dropped down and a few seconds later the deafening sound of stone crashing into life was again reverberating around the cave.

"Hang on to the rope but don't pull until the entrance is fully open," Columbus instructed.

When it did they pulled with all their might and sure enough the sword popped back up again. Clattering into Hudson's frame and plunging into the water they all momentarily lost their grip as the heavy sword sunk beneath the water.

"Quick pull it out, pull it out," Columbus urged them.

With one eye on the prize and another on edging back through the entrance to the tunnel, which was now closing again, all their eyes lit up as the glistening blade emerged from the water and then was pulled up on to the floor of the cave.

They passed the rope as quickly as they could through their hands sending the sword skipping from left to right as it bounced along the ground towards them.

"Stand back from the doors, Columbus," Drake warned her brother as he edged between them.

"Nearly there, it's nearly there," Columbus shouted, ignoring her.

"Stand back from the doors, Columbus," she shouted again but he was too intent on getting the sword.

Suddenly as the sword made its final dive to the entrance Drake pulled her brother back just as the cave doors crashed together with an almighty clanging sound.

Drake was the first to say something. "Is everyone all right?"

"I think we just killed the sword," Columbus replied solemnly.

"That was what that clanging sound was," Hudson sighed.

"Oh well there goes your find of the year," Professor Pinter added. "To tell you the truth I'm just glad to be in one piece. Those stone doors are something else. By the way who has got the torch?"

There was silence in the darkness.

"Don't tell me the rucksacks are on the other side," Professor Pinter groaned.

"Well we didn't really have any hands free did we," Columbus replied.

"Hold on to each other," Drake said and they all grabbed hold of another person's hand.

In the pitch black the group made their way alongside one of the walls of the tunnel very slowly until, after a good few minutes, they came to a brick wall.

"Blast, the way's blocked," Columbus said, as he felt along the bricks in the hope of finding a way out. "Hang on a minute some of these bricks are loose."

He pushed them forward firmly, sending them flying out of the wall and revealing several shafts of light in their place.

"Hurrah for that," Drake cried out. "I thought we were in here forever."

A few more bricks pushed out and there was enough space for all of them to climb from the tunnel and back out into the open.

Chapter Twenty-Five

Outside, the four took a deep breath of what was to them the most wonderful fresh air and then after a few minutes regaining their composure, took a look around at their surroundings.

To their surprise they found themselves below the dark, dank bridge that ran underneath the railway line.

"Hey I recognise this place," Hudson declared. "All we have to do is go back up there and we'll find the riverside path that takes us back to the station."

"And back home in time for tea," Columbus added looking at his watch.

They hurried out from beneath the dark, gravely path that led from under the bridge and stepped into the lighter shaded area of the path.

The fresh salty smell of the estuary hit them straight away and sure enough the seagulls and the site of the river drifting away in the distance told them exactly where they were.

Turn right and they would be back along the river to the

old Cathwella village. Left was the way home, via Wivenhoe station.

All of them had had enough adventure for one day and decided left was best.

Strolling along the path Drake sighed. "I'm glad we're out in the open."

"Yeah but what an adventure," Columbus added.

"I would rather we forgot the whole episode," Professor Pinter suddenly said.

"Are you kidding?" Columbus replied astonished by what the professor had just said. "If there ever was a story to go on the front page of Archaeology Today this has got to be it."

Professor Pinter frowned. "Dragons, a magic sword, not to mention assaults on unknown personages and a death," he said.

"Yeah but that was The Pole, he doesn't count," Hudson interrupted him.

"You, young man were the worst culprit. How many did you injure? And we still don't know what happened to the bloke who fell off the bridge."

Hudson sneered at the professor. "They deserved it, they were the baddies. Baddies always get it in the most unpleasant of ways."

"Look if you lot want to make fools of yourselves, then by all means call up the offices of Archaeology Today and tell them everything that has happened. They'll want proof though."

"But we all saw it with our own eyes," Columbus protested.

"But who is going to believe you?" Professor Pinter replied smiling. "No, you can leave me out of this one. I have a reputation to uphold."

They soon reached the nettles and bushes that barred their way to the station car park and after trampling a way through they trotted along to the ticket office.

Professor Pinter bought a single straight back home to

Wellsbridge while Columbus rummaged through his pockets.

"I haven't got any money," he told the others.

"Well don't look at me," Hudson replied. "I never have so much as a bean on me."

They both turned to Drake.

"Sorry," she replied.

"Can you lend us some money Pinter?" Columbus asked.

Professor Pinter was looking at the timetable to see when the next train out of Wivenhoe was.

"What was that?" he said.

"I was just wondering whether you could lend us some money," Columbus repeated.

The professor smiled. "No, I'm afraid not."

"But we haven't got enough to get home," Drake added.

"Looks like you'll have to walk then, or call your parents. I believe they are on a dig in Norfolk."

He smiled again, then turned round and made his way through the double doors and onto the platform.

"Well that didn't last very long," Drake said.

"What's that?" Hudson asked.

"Pinter being nice. Although I do think he gave us some good advice about the story in Archaeology Today."

"You think?" Columbus said.

"I do. No one is going to believe us when we tell them what happened. In fact they'll think we're mad. I still can't quite believe it myself," Drake shook her head. "No, I hate to say this but Pinter's right, without any proof it's just a rather good fairy story."

"Who said we haven't got any proof," Hudson spoke up from a seat in the far corner of the ticket office.

"What did you say?" Columbus asked him.

"I said, who said we haven't got any proof."

Drake and Columbus looked at each other bemused with what Hudson was trying to tell them.

"You mean we have?" Drake said.

Hudson nodded and then called his brother and sister over to where he was sitting.

"Over here, I don't want Pinter to hear this."

Drake and Columbus hurried to where he was and with a nod of the head Hudson directed their eyes to what was hanging around his neck.

It was his camera.

"Hudson, I could kiss you," Columbus announced with glee.

Hudson grimaced. "I'd rather you didn't."

The End

'Now you've read the story follow in the Young Explorers footsteps with the map of their expedition on the next page. Remember to watch out for dragons!'

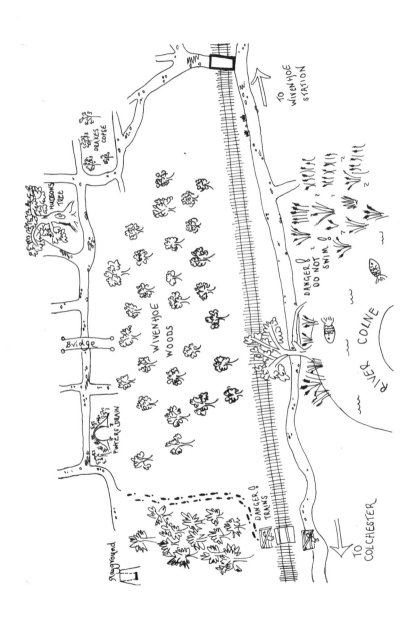

TO WIVENHOE STATION

DRAKES COPSE

HUDSONS TREE

Bridge

WIVENHOE WOODS

PINKERS DRAIN

DANGER DO NOT SWIM

RIVER COLNE

DANGER TRAINS

playground

TO COLCHESTER

THE YOUNG EXPLORERS TRAIL

Be a proper Young Explorer and get to Wivenhoe Station by train.

Wivenhoe is located on the Clacton and Walton branch line and best reached by Colchester North Station, located on the main London to Norwich line.

There is, however, a very good car park at the Wivenhoe Station and it is right next to the start of the trail.

Like Columbus, Drake and Hudson, start your walk at the far end of the station car park where fortunately there are no bramble bushes like there were in the Young Explorers' days.

Follow the gravel path for a few hundred metres and you will soon come across the railway bridge that leads into the woods.

Just like Hudson and Drake, steer well clear of the bridge and continue on the path.

With the railway line on your right and lines of trees on your left you will soon see the River Colne meander its way up close to the path.

Now you need to look out for those trees that bend over into the water where both Drake and the boys at the start of the book clambered onto and jumped into the river.

Don't forget what happened to them so stick to the path.

Another few hundred metres along the track where the river turns away from you there is the stretch of grass on the left where the Young Explorers stopped and tucked into Aunt Julia's packed lunch.

Why don't you have a bite to eat here as well.

Next it's up a small incline and then into some deep dark woods but don't worry you'll come out into the open again before going into some even deeper, darker woods.

They only last for a few metres as well and then you will find the stile round to the right which you need to go over to cross the railway.

Now make sure you look both left and right and take great care when crossing the railway line because on some days it can get quite busy.

Once over the line you will find yourself in a rather large area of parkland.

Up the hill and to the left you will find a playground. This wasn't there in the Young Explorers day but is where the ancient Cathwella village was located and where Columbus, Drake and Hudson camped out overnight.

No camping is allowed these days so bearing right away from the playground and towards Wivenhoe Woods you now need to go into the woods themselves.

As you get to the outskirts of the woods you should find a stony track which leads up to a row of houses. Just before the houses you will see a narrow path on your right which will lead you down to Pinter's Drain.

Past the drain on your right go up a hill and you will come into an opening with paths leading left, right and straight on.

Go straight on and you will come to the bridge which in the book was destroyed by a raging torrent but today is thankfully mended and crosses a very tiny stream.

Across the bridge you follow the path in a fairly straight line and while there are plenty of paths going off to the left it is the final one that branches off to the left where you will see Hudson's tree standing in between the two paths.

Continue straight on and eventually you will come to another crossway of paths where you go right.

That will take you round to a small mounded area which drops quite steeply down to your right. Opposite is the copse of trees where Drake, and the rest of the team found their secret tunnel.

You can look and try and find it yourself but lots of people have tried and failed.

If I was you I would take the right hand fork and follow the trail down some steps, out into the open back along the railway line, now on your right, and eventually you will come to a shady area with paths going off to the left, straight on and back to your right.

To the right you will see the railway bridge where Columbus, Drake, Hudson and Pinter finally emerged from their underground adventure.

Again you can try and find where the opening was but I'm told it was fixed and blocked in years ago.

Go under the bridge and rejoin the main path, remembering to turn left to get back to the station car park.

Happy Exploring!